SLICK ROCK CO'

Slick Rock 1

Becca Van

MENAGE EVERLASTING

Siren Publishing, Inc.
www.SirenPublishing.com

A SIREN PUBLISHING BOOK
IMPRINT: Ménage Everlasting

SLICK ROCK COWBOYS
Copyright © 2012 by Becca Van

ISBN-10: 1-61926-610-5
ISBN-13: 978-1-61926-610-0

First Printing: January 2012

Cover design by Les Byerley
All art and logo copyright © 2012 by Siren Publishing, Inc.

Printed in the U.S.A.

PUBLISHER
Siren Publishing, Inc.
www.SirenPublishing.com

DEDICATION

I would to thank all the staff of Siren-BookStrand for the opportunity to work with them. A special thanks to Diana, Erin, Kristen, and Lena for all the help in making my dreams come true. I couldn't have done it without you.

SLICK ROCK COWBOYS

Slick Rock 1

BECCA VAN
Copyright © 2012

Chapter One

Tara got off the bus after a long, hard day. Her feet were aching and so was her lower back after spending eight hours on her feet behind the counter of the delicatessen in her local supermarket. It didn't pay much, but at least it was a job. Tara turned the corner of her street and froze in her tracks. She saw fire trucks, flashing lights, and smelled the stench of smoke in the air. She gave a cry of alarm and began to run. She didn't even register that her flat slip-on shoes flew from her feet in her panic.

Tara Rustle stood outside in the street, staring at her apartment building. Flames erupted from the windows of the building, and glass and fire exploded out, making her jump as the whooshing and roaring of the fire reached her ears. She was thankful she was too far away to get hurt from the flying shards of glass. She remembered all the good times she and her mom had after they had moved from the small rural town of Slick Rock to Denver, Colorado. Her mind drifted back over that morning and the previous years of her life as she stood watching her life and what little of her mom's life she had kept go up in flames and smoke.

Tara had woken that morning to realize it was her birthday and gave a sigh of resignation knowing she would be spending her twenty-third birthday alone. Not that this birthday was any different from the last five, but she was sick and tired of being lonely. Sure, she had lots of acquaintances and even went out every now and then with some of the girls from work, but she didn't have any true best friends. Not anymore, anyway. She had left her only true friends behind at the tender age of fifteen.

When her dad had up and left her and her mom, Tara's mom had sold their ranch in Slick Rock, Colorado, and moved them both to Denver. Tara had felt as if her heart had been ripped out of her chest, broken in two, at having to leave her two best friends, Clay and Johnny Morten, behind. They had been neighbors ever since she could remember, and she had followed those two boys around like a lost puppy. Most of the time they tolerated her presence and had treated her like a kid sister, but as they had been quite a few years older than her, by the time she had left they were spending less and less time with her.

Clay had been twenty years old and Johnny eighteen. They had been chasing girls and had girls chasing them, much to Tara's dismay. Tara had had a crush on the two boys ever since she was twelve years old, and the day she had wandered over to the Double M Ranch and found the two young men in the barn sharing a woman was the day Tara had felt her heart break in two. They had never even known she was there. She had crept into the barn and seen them with that slutty Chantal from the diner. Tara had gone over to tell her friends she was leaving Slick Rock in less than a week, but she never got the chance. In fact, she had never seen those two boys again.

Tara's mom had sold their run-down ranch, and since most of their stuff had been pawned off for food and bills, there had not been much to do in the way of packing. Tara and her mom had left their home three days later. They had ended up in Denver, Colorado, and two years later, Tara's mom was dead. She had been struck by a car on her way home from work one night. Tara had been in the process of cooking dinner, waiting for her mom to come home so she could serve it up, when there had been a knock on the door.

Tara had been so scared to find the law on her doorstep, and when they had asked to come inside, she knew, deep down, something had happened to her mom. Tara had been thankful her mom had paid a little each week for life insurance, which had been enough to cover the expenses for her mom's funeral and all of the other incidentals that had been involved. Tara had never really had the time to grieve properly for her mom. She'd had to push everything to the back of her mind and search for a job to keep a roof over her head, food in her belly, and some clothes on her back.

As much as Tara loved Colorado, Denver had never felt like home to her. She missed her childhood home of Slick Rock. She wanted nothing more than to pack up and go back to her childhood roots. She had saved a little money each week, enough to live on for about a month if necessary, but nowhere near enough to move home from Denver to Slick Rock.

Tara had blown out the candle on the small cupcake she had bought the previous evening on her way home from work and had made a heartfelt wish. She was too old and cynical to believe wishes came true anymore, but her inner child would not let go of her childhood dreams. Tara had wiped the tears from her cheeks and eaten her small cake for breakfast then gone to shower and gotten ready for work.

* * * *

"Miss, are you all right? Did you have any family inside?" the officer asked in concern.

The sound of the police officer's voice pulled her from her reverie. How long Tara had stood there staring in shock, she had no idea. It wasn't until the young police officer walked over to her and asked her if she was all right that she finally came out of her stupor.

Tara stared in horror as a grumbling, roaring noise drew her attention back to her burning home. She was just in time to see her apartment building's roof cave in, flames billowing high into the night sky. Then the whole building came tumbling down to the ground. .

"No. No family," Tara replied in a croaky voice.

"Are you sure you're all right? Can I call someone for you?"

"No. There's no one," Tara replied then turned around after one last look at her burning home and disappeared into the night.

* * * *

Tara jolted awake as the bus she was on slowed and then stopped with a hiss of air brakes. She rubbed her tired, sore eyes and hoped she didn't look as bad as she felt. She had no idea where she was. She couldn't remember getting on a bus. *What the hell am I doing here?* Tara picked up her purse and stood up. It was only then she realized her feet were cold and bare. *Where the hell are my shoes?* She rubbed her forehead as she tried to remember what she was doing, but for the life of her she couldn't remember. She got off the bus, moved across the parking lot and through the small bus terminal.

Tara stood out on the sidewalk and stared about her. Some of the shops and the town looked familiar, but she couldn't place where she had seen it before. She rubbed a hand across her eyes and took a few more steps. She was going to have to cross the street to get to the cafe on the other side for some much-needed food. She couldn't remember the last time she had eaten.

Tara stood in the middle of the road as she waited for the traffic to clear. She felt so dizzy she thought she was going to throw up and pass out. She tried to clear the fog from her eyes but was not successful. She could hear a roaring sound in her ears, and a cold sweat popped out all over her body. She could feel herself falling, but couldn't seem to do a thing about it. Darkness formed in front of her eyes, and her ears were ringing. She pitched forward and slid into unconsciousness.

Chapter Two

Johnny looked over to Clay as they finished loading their truck with some horse and cattle feed. Since it was lunchtime, they decided to drive on over to the diner for a meal instead of going home and having their usual sandwiches. Since their last housekeeper had left a month ago, the two brothers had had to put up with their own miserable cooking, and they were getting mighty tired of eating charcoal or half-raw food. They lived mostly on canned food and toasted sandwiches. Every time they tried to cook, the food almost always ended up in the trash and they would end up having toasted sandwiches, as usual. They really needed to get a housekeeper, or at least a cook, and fast.

"Clay, watch out," Johnny yelled as he watched a bedraggled woman with bare feet fall into the middle of the road, right in front of their approaching truck.

Johnny reached for the dashboard to hold himself steady when Clay stomped on the brake pedal and brought the truck to a screeching halt in the middle of the road. He put the stick into neutral, pulled on the parking brake. Johnny heard Clay's footsteps following behind him as they rushed to help the fallen woman.

Johnny got to the woman before Clay and knew his brother watched as he picked the slight female up into his arms, carried her off the road, and headed for the diner. Johnny froze in the doorway of the diner, staring down into the woman's thin face, while Clay held the door open for him.

"Tara," Johnny whispered, knowing his brother had heard him when he saw Clay move closer in his peripheral vision to look at the woman in his arms.

"Oh my God. It is Tara," Clay confirmed as the brothers stared down at the woman who had haunted their dreams for the last eight years.

Johnny and Clay jumped as a car horn sounded, and Clay ran to the truck to get it out of the middle of the road. Johnny carried Tara into the diner and sat down carefully, pulling her onto his lap, making sure to support her slight body with his own. He looked up to see Clay rushing through the door of the diner then looked back down to the woman moaning in his arms. Tara was just coming around as Clay sat on the seat across from him. Maisie, the owner of the diner, brought out a clean washcloth, as well as some water and ice.

Johnny was wiping what looked like soot off of Tara's face with the damp cloth, and then he brushed her blonde hair away from her face. She was rail thin and as pale as a ghost. It looked like the slightest breeze would push her over. She gave a low moan just before her eyes fluttered open.

Johnny stared into the green eyes which had taunted him and his brother when they were younger, and he watched as their woman began to come around. She was their woman, had been since she was fourteen years old. He and Johnny had just been waiting for her to grow up. Johnny and Clay had felt like perverts lusting after their young neighbor, and had begun having sex with any willing female just to keep control of themselves while they waited for her.

"Are you all right, sweetheart?" Johnny asked.

"Where am I? Who are you?" she asked with a frown, rubbing her hand over her forehead as if trying to bring her memory back.

"You're in Slick Rock, Colorado. What happened to you? What's your name?" Johnny asked as he watched Tara through narrowed eyes suspiciously. He wasn't sure if she was faking, not wanting to be with them. She had never even said good-bye when she left Slick Rock. All the resentment and bitterness Johnny had been feeling over the years came to the surface. He had to clench his jaw to prevent himself from railing at her.

"Um, I…I can't remember. Where's my purse?" Tara asked, moving off the man's lap to sit beside him as she looked around then out the window to the road.

"Here, why don't you have a drink of water, honey? I'm Maisie, I own and run this here diner. These two men are Johnny and Clay Morten. They'll take real good care of you." Maisie sat down next to Clay and pushed the glass across the table.

"Thank you."

"Can you remember how you got to Slick Rock? You didn't have a purse on you when you passed out in the middle of the road," Clay replied.

* * * *

Tara sat up in her seat and stared at the man next to her and the other one across the table from her. She felt as if she ought to know them, but how could that be? She didn't even know where she was.

She looked at the handsome man sitting across from her. Clay had collar-length black hair and light-green eyes and looked to be around thirty years old. She could tell he was tall, about six foot three at a guess, even though he was sitting down. He had a square jaw, a little sexy indentation in his chin, and high cheekbones. He wore only denim blue jeans and a T-shirt beneath his open flannel shirt. She could see his muscles rippling beneath his shirt as he moved. Her eyes slid away from his body over to his brother, Johnny. He was just as handsome, with similar familial features, except his hair was dark brown instead of black, and his eyes were hazel. She could see small flecks of gold mixed in with the brown and green. He was taller than his brother and a couple of years younger. He was slightly wider across the chest and shoulders than Clay, more muscular. Johnny seemed to be less intense than Clay, his body language more relaxed.

"Bus, I think. Yes, I came here on a bus. I'm sure I had my purse with me."

"Excuse me, honey, I need to go and serve some customers. Clay, come on over and order your lunch," Maisie ordered, rising to her feet and moving toward the counter, Clay at her heels.

Tara watched as Clay moved away to the counter of the diner with Maisie. She could see them talking but couldn't hear what they said because they were too far away.

* * * *

"I think you need to take that little gal down to Doc Foster. She looks mighty unwell to me. But before you do, we'll fill her belly with some good food. You want the usual?" Maisie asked.

"Yeah, thanks, Maisie. Can you call Doc and set up an appointment for us after lunch? Me and Johnny will make sure she gets down to Doc's place," Clay stated as he glanced over his shoulder back at the table. He was about to turn back when he watched her familiar move of brushing her hair back behind her ear.

The pain he felt when she had first left all those years ago reared its ugly head and stabbed him in the heart. Why had she left without telling them where she was going? Why had she not written to them and let them know she was all right?

"Clay, you all right, honey? You look like you've just seen a ghost," Maisie asked from behind him.

"Yeah, I'm okay. Just remembered something from the past. Don't worry about it, Maisie, just being fanciful is all." Clay handed over the money for the three lunch orders.

"This one's on me, young man. No, don't argue. Not many people left these days that would help out a stranger."

"Thanks, Maisie," Clay replied, not willing to go into the details about Tara not being a stranger. He just felt too raw to be opening up with anyone just yet.

"Go on, I'll call the Doc then bring your food out."

Clay sat down at the table and watched as Johnny interacted with Tara. He couldn't get it out of his head that he was finally actually sitting at a table across from their long-lost neighbor, and she had no idea who they were. He wanted nothing more than to call out her name, but was hesitant. She could be faking not remembering who she was, but if she wasn't and had some type of amnesia, he could end up damaging their woman even more.

Johnny and Clay cajoled Tara into eating the plate of food Maisie had placed in front of her. They tried to get her to eat all the food, but she told them if she ate more than the half she had eaten she would make herself sick. Clay worried over that, because he knew she never used to worry about her weight when she was younger, not that she'd ever needed to. Clay wondered just how long it had been since she'd had a decent meal.

Once they'd all finished eating, Johnny and Clay each took her by the elbow and steered her to their truck.

"Wait. Where are you taking me?" Tara asked nervously.

Clay watched as she glanced around, and he could see how nervous she was. She was gripping one hand with the other, her knuckles white.

"We are taking you to see a doctor, sweetheart. We want to make sure you're all right. After that, if you like, you can come and stay at our ranch. We are in need of a cook and housekeeper and thought you might like to work after you've rested up some. That way you'll have a roof over your head and food in your belly until your memory returns or if you just decide you want to move on again," Johnny said in a quiet, calm voice.

The last thing Clay wanted to do was scare Tara and have her run again. Clay and his brother had just about resigned themselves to the fact they would never see their woman again. Clay had discussed the issue with Johnny and had decided to push Tara from their hearts and minds and try to get on with their lives. Now that she was back in their clutches again, there was no fucking way he was letting her leave. But first he and Johnny had to find out if she was really sick or if not, what sort of game she was playing.

* * * *

Clay pulled into the parking lot in front of Doc's, walked around his truck, and helped Johnny steer Tara into the office. They didn't have to wait as Doc Foster had a gap and took Tara into his consulting room right away.

"Hi there, Miss, I'm Doc Foster, but everyone around these parts calls me Doc. Now what can I do for you?"

"I–I don't know. I can't remember anything," Tara sobbed.

"There, there now," Doc said in a calm voice as he rubbed the distraught woman's back. "Why don't you go behind that curtain, put on the gown, and I'll check you over when you give me a holler?"

"Okay," Tara whispered then gave an inelegant sniff. She grabbed a few tissues from the box on Doc's desk and disappeared behind the curtain.

"Okay. I'm ready," Tara called out after a few moments.

Clay watched as Doc checked Tara over thoroughly, making sure she didn't have any bumps or lumps on her head with his fingertips. He checked her blood pressure and monitored her heart with his stethoscope. Clay realized he couldn't find anything when a puzzled expression crossed his face. It was a different story when Doc checked her pupils. Doc checked the reaction of her eyes time and again until he finally put the pen light back into his coat pocket. Even Clay could tell her pupils were very sluggish and slow to respond. Clay saw Doc give Tara a pat on the arm as he moved away and closed the curtain so she could dress.

"You get dressed, now. I'll be back in a minute," Doc called out and exited the consulting room, Clay on his heels.

"How is she, Doc?" asked Clay.

"That's Tara Rustle, isn't it?" Doc asked as he looked from Clay to Johnny.

"Yeah, we were on our way to the diner after picking up some stock feed and I nearly ran over her as she collapsed in the middle of the road. What's wrong with her, Doc?" Clay asked.

"She's undernourished and slightly dehydrated. It looks like she hasn't eaten properly in months. She is also suffering from deep shock. I don't know what's happened to her, but whatever it is, her mind couldn't handle it and it's shut down on her."

"She couldn't be fakin' it, could she?" Johnny asked the question before Clay could.

"No. Her pupils are really sluggish. If I hadn't checked her over and seen for myself she has no bumps or lumps on her head, I would have thought she had a head injury. She is going to need to eat and rest for the next few days. Hopefully, once she's feeling more herself, her memory will come back of its own accord. Just be careful with her. I know you two boys have had a hankering for that woman for more years than I can count. And I know you never touched her while she was still a child, but I know you aren't going to let her go this time. Just go real slow with her, or you could be doing more damage than good. Bring her back to see me if you think she needs some help," Doc Foster stated then left the empty waiting room.

Tara came back into the waiting room five minutes later and stood hesitantly as she eyed Clay and Johnny nervously, biting on her lower lip as she shifted from foot to foot.

"Are you okay, sweetheart?" Johnny asked as he moved toward her.

"Yes," Tara replied quietly.

"Do you remember if you had any luggage with you, baby?" Clay asked as he, too, moved up beside Tara.

"Uh, I...I can't remember," Tara replied with a hitch in her voice.

"Well, that's okay. Don't you worry about it now. We need to get you home so you can rest up. We'll figure something out later. Come on," Clay urged as he grasped one of her elbows and Johnny took the other.

They led her out to the truck, saw her comfortably and safely buckled in, then began the trek back to the ranch.

Tara was asleep moments later.

Chapter Three

Tara was on her feet beside the bed about to head to the bathroom and yawned as she stretched and blinked the sleep from her eyes. She looked around the strange room as she stood beside the bed and wondered who had removed her clothes. She was completely naked. She grabbed for the comforter on the bed and pulled it to cover her body when she heard footsteps outside the bedroom door. She clutched the cover to her chest and gave a squeak of surprise as the door to the bedroom opened and Clay and Johnny walked into the room.

"Are you all right, babe?" Clay asked.

Tara watched warily as he walked over to the bed and sat down on the edge of the mattress.

"Yes. Where am I?"

"You're on our ranch. Don't you remember? We took you to Doc's, and then we were bringing you back here. You fell asleep in the truck before we got home," Clay advised.

"Do you want a drink, sweetheart?" Johnny asked as he held up a full glass of water.

"Please."

Tara reached for the glass Johnny handed over and guzzled down the water. She hadn't even realized how thirsty she was until she started drinking.

"Why do you keep calling me babe and sweetheart?" Tara asked in a disgruntled voice when she'd finished her water.

"What do you want us to call you?" Clay asked.

"Um, ah, shit."

"Don't worry about it, sweetheart. It will come back to you when you least expect it. The more you try and force your memory, the harder it will be. Just relax," Johnny stated calmly.

"Who undressed me?" Tara asked, fire creeping up over her cheeks as she lowered her eyes.

"We both did, babe. We didn't want you to be uncomfortable, and your clothes were pretty grubby. Johnny will go shopping for you later and pick out some clothes so you have a few things until you want to get some more clothes. We're just waiting until you feel up to going shopping for yourself. I'll bet you'd like a bath or a shower right now, so why don't you take one while we organize some dinner?" Clay suggested.

"Okay. I would kill for a bath, and thanks so much for taking care of me. I don't know what I would have done if you two hadn't come along," Tara said with a quiet voice.

"Hey, you're doing us a favor, remember? We're getting a cook and maybe a housekeeper out of this, but not until you feel well enough. So for the next couple of days you'll have to put up with canned food and toasted sandwiches," Johnny said and gave her a wink.

She watched as they left, closing the door behind them. She gave a sigh of frustration at having no memories, but since there was nothing she could do about it, she headed to the bathroom.

* * * *

Tara luxuriated at feeling clean once again after she had washed her hair and body. She scrounged under the vanity and found a toothbrush still in its packaging, as well as some toothpaste. She scrubbed her teeth and gargled some mouthwash. She felt nearly human once again instead of something the cat had dragged in from the garden. She found a large white T-shirt draped over a chair in the bedroom and, since that was all she could find to wear, pulled it on then walked down the long hallway.

Tara stopped in the doorway of the kitchen, watching the two large men moving about the room. Clay was getting coffee mugs down while Johnny made dinner. The smell of toasted cheese sandwiches made her stomach growl loudly. She didn't think it had been that loud, but must have been loud enough to alert the two tall, sexy cowboys to her presence. They turned to look at her at the same time. Tara's cheeks heated, and she lowered her eyes when she caught the heat in their eyes as they perused her body covered only in the large white T-shirt.

"Come in and take a seat, sweetheart. Dinner's almost done," Johnny said from across the room.

"Um, do either of you have a robe or something I could borrow, please?" Tara asked quietly, still standing in the doorway.

"Are you cold, sweetheart?" asked Johnny.

"No, not really, but I don't feel comfortable wearing only a T-shirt."

"That T-shirt never looked that good on me, baby. But if you're uncomfortable I'll grab you a robe," Clay advised, his voice husky as his eyes once again wandered the length of her body, and then he turned and left. He was back in moments and handed Tara a robe.

"I'm just used to more clothes," Tara replied as she pulled the robe on. "Thanks for the robe."

"Come and sit down and eat while your sandwiches are still hot. Sorry it's not much of a meal, but we can't cook," Johnny stated with a grin as he placed a plate on the table. When she didn't move, he walked over to her, took one of her hands, and led her to the table. He pulled out a chair and eased her down onto it.

Tara looked at the pile of sandwiches and wondered if she was supposed to eat them all. There was no way she would be able to eat two of them, let alone the four on the plate in front of her. She picked up half a sandwich and bit into it, keeping her eyes lowered to the table. She finished eating and swayed in her chair as the image of a building burning and falling to the ground flashed through her mind. She gripped the edge of the chair she was sitting on as nausea rolled through her stomach. She took several deep breaths and swallowed as she tried to fight her sick stomach. Her stomach was roiling, and she knew she had to move, and quickly, or she would end up disgracing herself in front of her new employers by throwing up. She pushed her chair back, dizziness assailing her as she raced stumbling from the room. Tara made it to the bathroom just in time to empty the contents of her stomach.

* * * *

Clay and Johnny entered the bathroom just in time to catch Tara as she went down falling to the floor after losing her dinner. Clay picked her supine form up in his arms and carried her to the bedroom. He stripped the robe and T-shirt from her body as he ordered Johnny to collect a bowl of warm water and a washcloth.

Clay washed Tara's white, clammy face and then set about washing the rest of her body. She was covered in sweat, and he began to worry when she didn't wake up.

"Johnny, call Doc Foster's, and see if he can come out to check her over. I don't care how much it costs, our little darlin' is sick," he said as he patted Tara's skin dry. He pulled a clean T-shirt out of a drawer and pulled it over her head, arms, and shoulders. He half lifted her and pulled the shirt down to cover the thin body.

"Doc will be here in about ten minutes. He was on his way home, thank God. What do you think that was all about?" Johnny asked with concern as he studied Tara's pale face.

"I have no idea, but we will soon enough." He sat down on the edge of the bed and smoothed Tara's hair back off her face. Her color was starting to come back, which was a good sign. He didn't want to leave her in case she was sick while she was still asleep.

"Why don't you go finish dinner? There's nothing we can do until

Doc gets here. When you're done, you can sit with her and I'll finish eating. On second thought, why don't you just bring our plates in here and we can both watch over her till Doc gets here?" Clay asked, knowing his brother was not willing to leave their girl while she was sick.

Clay gave a nod of appreciation when Johnny handed him his dinner. He moved his legs up onto the bed, resting his back up against the headboard. He couldn't keep his eyes off their woman. She was so sexy, even though she was way too skinny. He planned to change that as soon as he could. Their woman had been to hell and back. It frustrated the hell out of Clay not knowing what had happened to her. He was never letting her out of his sight again. No matter what.

Clay had just finished his dinner as he heard Doc knock on the door. He watched Johnny leave the room to take their plates back to the kitchen and let Doc into the house. Clay eyed Doc as he and Johnny entered the room just in time to see Tara open her eyes. He saw her glance around her and watched as embarrassment tinged her cheeks a red hue.

"How are you feeling, young lady?" asked Doc, moving further into the room.

"Okay. Could I have a drink of water please?"

Clay nearly laughed as Johnny took off in a hurry and was back in moments with a jug full of water and a glass. He watched as his brother poured her a drink and handed it to her. He glanced over at Doc, and he saw the look of satisfaction on the elderly man's face as Tara drank the whole glass down.

"Now what seems to be the problem? These two boys are worried sick about you. They called me saying you'd been sick and fainted."

"Um…" Tara hesitated as she looked to Clay and Johnny from beneath her lowered eyelashes.

"How 'bout you boys go and make me some coffee? I could certainly use a cup after the long day I've had," Doc Foster said to Clay, and he knew the man wanted him and Johnny out of the room.

He and Johnny waited in the kitchen impatiently as they set about brewing a fresh pot of coffee. Clay and his brother had known the elderly man since they had been knee high to a grass hopper. He knew the first thing Doc would do when he entered the kitchen would be to get a clean mug from the cupboard.

"What's wrong with her, Doc?" Clay asked as soon as Doc entered the kitchen.

"Tara's memory is beginning to return. She had a flash of a building burning to the ground. Normally a person wouldn't be sick, the dizziness I can understand. That little girl has been through emotional hell. You need to keep an eye on her. Her full memory could return at any moment, and I don't know how she is going to handle that," Doc stated with a frown.

"You don't think she'd try and harm herself, do you?" Clay asked through a voice tight with emotion.

"I don't know. I just don't know. I want one of you with her all the time. Hire someone to help you out with the ranch and take over some of your chores, and for goodness sakes, get that girl some clothes."

"I'm going into town for clothes tomorrow," Johnny replied.

"Good, get her these vitamins while you're there. It will help with her appetite and build her strength up again," Doc said as he passed over the note. "Now, I'm heading home. Call me if you need to."

"You don't want a coffee before you go?" Clay asked.

"No," Doc replied, "Thanks anyway, but I just want to get on home."

"Thanks, Doc," Clay replied as he saw the older man to the door. Once back inside, Clay got on the phone, intending to do what Doc had said. He was hiring some ranch hands to take over all the work. There was no way in hell they were leaving Tara alone. No way were they letting her do something stupid.

Chapter Four

Tara was feeling so much better since she had slept for nearly fifteen hours. She showered and dressed in another clean T-shirt then searched through the cupboards and closet until she found the robe she'd worn the night before. Feeling much better with another layer over the shirt, she rolled the sleeves to the robe up and entered the kitchen.

Tara put on the coffeepot and began to get breakfast. By the time she heard the shower running down the hall, she was just finishing up the scrambled eggs, bacon, and toast. She placed the food in a dish in the oven to keep it warm until the two men came to eat.

"Hey, sweetheart, how are you feeling?" Johnny asked as he wrapped his arms around Tara's waist from behind and planted a kiss on her temple.

"I'm fine," Tara squeaked out as she held herself stiffly in his arms.

Johnny gave a sigh and released Tara. He poured himself a coffee and sat at the table. "You're not supposed to be doing any chores yet. Doc said you're supposed to rest."

"I've had more than enough resting in the last two days to last me a lifetime. I wanted to get up and make you and your brother breakfast. That's what I'm here for, remember? I can't just lay about the place when I've decided to accept the job to cook and clean for you."

"I don't care what we hired you for, baby. If you're not up to doing anything, then don't. We don't want you getting sick again," Clay stated in a firm voice, his eyes shooting daggers at her.

"I'm much better, thanks, Clay. I wouldn't have cooked if I wasn't," Tara replied as she thrust her chin out at him.

Tara knew Clay was fighting back a smile because she could see the muscle in his jaw flexing as he bit down hard. Tara was beginning to feel a little more like herself. Her gumption was returning. There was no way she was letting Clay and his brother run roughshod over her. She just knew there were going to be fireworks between them. They felt so familiar to her. She was beginning to feel as if she had known them her whole life. But she had to set some ground rules if she was going to be living with the two sexy men. Somehow, she knew deep inside, she wasn't the sort of person to be pushed around. She couldn't be anyone other than herself. Even though she wasn't really sure about who she was, she had a feeling she was usually pretty feisty, and there was no way she was letting these two dominant men control her.

Tara got breakfast out of the oven and placed it on the table. She'd already set the table, so she had nothing else to do. She poured herself another cup of coffee and sat down to eat.

"I'm going into town today to pick up a few things," Johnny said as he looked at Tara. "Is there anything I can get you?"

"Yes. Do you have a charity shop in town?"

"Yeah. Why?"

"I was wondering if you could get me some clothes and you can take it out of my first paycheck?" Tara muttered as she lowered her eyes, heat racing up to cover her cheeks.

"You won't be wearing secondhand clothes, baby. Johnny's going to get you some this morning. No. Don't you dare argue. You need clothes. You can't go around wearing our T-shirts all the time. As much as we like the way you look in them, you need some decent clothes. I'll take a little out of your paycheck each week to cover the cost. Okay?" Clay asked rhetorically.

"Thank you, so much," Tara said in a voice that broke with emotion.

"Aw, babe. Come here," Clay said as he pushed back his chair and held a hand out to her.

Tara shook her head and sat quietly with her eyes lowered, and tears leaked out the corner of her eyes to course down her cheeks.

"Tara, look at me," Clay demanded.

Tara's head snapped up. She could feel her heart pounding hard against her breasts. Her skin went hot all over, and she felt perspiration break out. Then she went cold, not just skin cold. The cold went bone deep. She began to shake, her breath rasping out of her mouth. She felt sick to her stomach and felt as if all the blood drained from her face. Her memory came rushing back with a vengeance. Pain pierced her skull, and her arms rose as she gripped her head between her hands as the death of her mother, the struggle to survive, and the preceding years flashed across her brain. She remembered hanging around Clay and Johnny when she was kid. She had grown up with them. The horrid sight her young heart would never be able to comprehend came rushing back. She remembered walking in on Clay and Johnny fucking another woman. The loss of her mom and the uncertainty surrounding her father's disappearance years before, her home, her clothes, her precious photos of her mom all came rushing back. The memories hit her with such a force she fell from her chair to the floor. She doubled over, clutching her stomach as she began to sob.

* * * *

Clay swore under his breath, got off his chair, scooped Tara up into his arms, and pulled her onto his lap as he sat back down. He rocked and soothed her as she cried heart-wrenching sobs against his chest. He began to get worried when she didn't slow down. He looked over to Johnny to see a worried frown and sadness, which he knew was mirrored in his own eyes. Clay was beginning to be really concerned for Tara's health when her tears didn't let up.

He picked her up, gestured to Johnny to follow him to the bathroom. He handed Tara over to Johnny as he stripped out of his clothes and turned the shower on. He saw Johnny begin to strip Tara's clothes from her body as she leaned against his brother. He watched his brother kiss their woman tenderly on her head, and then he scooped her into his arms and stepped into the warm, soothing shower. He was grateful when the warm water began to soothe, warm, and calm Tara, and sighed with relief as Tara's tears slowed as did her sobs. He heard her hiccup a few times, and then she slumped down against his chest. Her breathing slowed until she was once again quiet and calm. Clay slid Tara down his naked body and helped to steady her on her feet. He tilted her head up to his and looked into her bloodshot, swollen, red-rimmed eyes.

"I'm sorry," Tara whispered then hid her face against Clay's chest and wrapped her arms around his waist.

Clay wouldn't let Tara back off as she tried to pull away. He slid his arms down her sides and held onto her hips firmly. His cock began to rise as Tara's little nipples stabbed into his chest as they rubbed against his chest hair and skin.

"Clay, please let me go."

"No," Clay replied as he reached the faucets, turned the water off, and scooped Tara into his arms. "I can't risk you falling down and hurting yourself, baby. You've exhausted yourself with your crying, you're unsteady on your feet and look ready to collapse." He held her still while Johnny dried her off, then grabbed a clean towel to dry himself as Johnny wrapped Tara up in the robe.

Clay quickly dressed as he watched Tara standing in front of him, glaring at him defiantly. Johnny's arms kept her still as he wrapped her within his embrace. Clay moved toward her, scooped her up into his arms, and headed back into the kitchen. He sat down and pulled Tara onto his lap, one of his large, muscular arms holding her around the waist like a steel band. He tilted her face up to his and stared down into her eyes.

"Talk to me, Tara. Tell me what's happened to you," Clay demanded, the muscle in his jaw flexing as he clenched his teeth.

"Nothing has happened to me."

"Bullshit. You aren't going anywhere until you start talking. I can sit here all day and night if I have to," Clay advised, emphasizing his statement with determination.

"Mom died when I was seventeen. She was hit by a car on her way home from work. I've been trying to make ends meet to pay for rent, bills, and food. I was working in a delicatessen, which was the only job I could get. It didn't pay enough. I barely had any money left for food by the time everything else way paid. I came home from work the other night to find my apartment building on fire and watched as it collapsed to the ground. Everything I owned went up in smoke. We didn't have any insurance because we couldn't afford it. I don't remember what happened after that. I...my mind must have snapped. The only thing I remember is waking up in the diner with you two trying to look after me."

"Aw, baby. Why didn't you come home, here to us?" Clay asked as he hugged her to him.

"Why would I want to do that? The last time I came to see you and Johnny, you were both too busy to even notice I was there," she responded, folding her arms beneath her breasts protectively.

"When was that? We were never too busy for you, sweetheart," Johnny said, a frown creasing his forehead.

"It doesn't matter."

"Don't you dare lie to us, Tara. I can hear it in your voice how much it doesn't matter," Clay ground out.

"Fuck it," Johnny yelled. "It was the day you left, wasn't it? You caught us in the barn fucking that woman. It didn't mean anything, Tara. We're a lot older than you, and you have to remember we were younger back then. Our hormones were running rampant. God, we can't even remember her name."

"Is that supposed to make it right?" Tara yelled at Johnny as she pushed off Clay's lap. "I saw you, both of you. I saw what you were doing to that woman, and now you have the gall to tell me you can't even remember her name? I can't believe you would use a female like that. My God…"

"Shut up, Tara. You don't know what you're talking about. You were too young to know what was going on," Clay said quietly.

"Do you know how I felt having to come and say good-bye to you two? Knowing I would probably never see you again? To find you fucking a woman, both at the same time? You knew I had a crush on the both of you. You broke my heart that day," Tara sobbed out then spun on her heels and ran from the room.

Clay stood staring at Johnny, not knowing what to do or say. He watched as Johnny turned his back on him, walked to the coffeepot, and poured himself a cup.

"Fuck it, Clay. Why did you have to call her by name? We could have tried to woo her back to us before her memory returned. I don't see how we can get her to stay with us now. What the hell are we going to do?" Johnny roared at his brother then hurled his coffee cup across the room. He stormed out of the kitchen, slamming the back door behind him.

Clay sank down on his chair and wiped a hand over his face. He'd really fucked up by not thinking before he spoke. He didn't know how they were going to keep Tara from running, but he knew they couldn't let her leave. He got up from his chair and stormed out of the kitchen, down the hall to the closed bedroom door. He raised his hand to knock, hesitated, then dropped his hand to his side. He walked out of the house, slammed his fist against the timber boards, cursing as pain radiated from his knuckles through his hand. He knew they had a bit of time before Tara left. She still had no clothes. He watched Johnny roar past in the truck as he headed to town. He would be waiting for his brother to return. He was going to have to give her the option of leaving, but he was going to try and get her to stay until she was fully recovered. He didn't want to let her go but knew he couldn't keep her against her will. No, he couldn't do that to the woman he loved. He was just going to have to try to get through to her that he and Johnny wanted to protect and help her. He couldn't let anything else happen to Tara. He loved her too much.

Chapter Five

Tara sat on the window seat in her room, her knees drawn up to her chest as she stared out into the yard. She was glad her memory was back, but her chest felt so tight with pain and despair. She wanted to leave, but had no clothes or money and nowhere to go. At least she had a roof over her head for now. If she left, she would end up living on the streets. As much as her pride demanded she leave, she wasn't stupid enough to give up the only place she had for now.

Tara had heard Johnny and Clay arguing but couldn't hear what they'd said. No doubt they had argued over her. She'd heard the crash of something smashing against the wall, the slam of the back door, and then the roar of an engine as one of the men, or maybe both, left the house. Tara sat up straight and lowered her feet to the floor, pushing her hair from her face. She needed to get herself together, organize the cancellation of her credit and ATM cards, since she had lost her purse and wallet, and then she was going to try and find herself a job.

Tara made her phone calls and gave the bank her temporary address. It would be at least two weeks before the bank would send her replacement cards. She went into the ranch office, grabbed the newspaper, and began to peruse the employment section. She picked up the pen to circle any appropriate jobs, found a pad of paper, and began to write letters. She addressed and stamped the letters and hoped Clay or Johnny would mail them for her. If not, she would borrow some clothes and do it herself. She needed to get out of here as soon as she could. There was no way she was hanging around to betray herself any more than she already had. She hoped Clay hadn't noticed her body's reaction when he'd taken her into the shower during her meltdown. She had a hard time keeping her eyes off of their hard, sexy bodies. Time and again she found her eyes drawn to their physiques. She was even aware when Clay had caught her in the act. He had given her a sexy half smile and wink, then given her the once-over as well. She had been independent for so long, and she was already beginning to lean on her two friends. She didn't like that she was becoming dependent on them so quickly.

Tara had never really made friends easily growing up, had spent all of her spare time doing chores, studying, reading, or hanging around Clay and Johnny. She'd always felt as if she were on the outside of a big bubble watching others interact in their perfect little worlds with their perfect friends. She knew now how immature those thoughts had been. Nobody in the world was perfect, and she knew there were others who had a lot worse childhood than she'd had. She had always been a shy, timid person. Her father was probably the main cause of that. He had always been angry. If he wasn't ranting and raving at her mom, he was busy working on the ranch or in the bottom of a bottle. He'd never hit her mom or her, though. Not that it excused his behavior. Tara had tried to make herself invisible to her father. She had been on the receiving end of his verbal abuse at the early age of eight years old. The only time she'd ever let herself be natural was around her mom when her dad was not home and around Johnny and Clay. They had coaxed her out of her shell, and she was grateful to them. Habits of a lifetime were hard to break, and to be honest with herself, she was just too scared to care for anyone anymore. Anyone she ever cared for always ended up leaving her, whether they wanted to or not. What was the point? She was better off alone. It hurt less that way.

Tara needed to get out of the house. She was going stir crazy and knew she wouldn't see Clay or Johnny for a while. She headed to the bedroom to rummage in the drawers and find herself something to wear. She looked at herself in the mirror, covered her mouth with her hand, and giggled. She looked ridiculous. The jeans she had borrowed were so big on her, if she hadn't found a belt and added more holes to it, the pants would be down around her ankles. The legs were rolled up so many times, it looked like her shins and calves were deformed. The jacket she had on over the large T-shirt hid her hands and wouldn't stay rolled up no matter what she did. The arms were too wide, and she had lost too much weight to keep the rolled fabric in place. Her hands were invisible beneath the floppy ends of the jacket. Tara gave a mental shrug and headed out the back door.

Tara breathed in the scent of the roses and jasmine planted just outside the back door. She wandered down to the corral and leaned on the fence as she took in the beautiful scenery. The expansive plains and fresh country air seeped into her soul, relaxing her for the first time in six years. She had missed her home so much, as well as her two best friends, but she missed her mom the most. She felt like a big, gaping wound had split her chest wide open and would never heal. She had lost the closeness of her best friends the day she moved away from this place, and two years later, she had lost her mom. She had no one anymore and didn't know if she would ever feel whole again.

The first sob caught Tara by surprise. She would have thought she had no tears left after all the crying she had done over the last couple of days. She slid to the ground and hugged her knees in tight to her chest. She felt so alone. She had no one to lean on, no one to love, and no one to love her in return. She had nothing left. Tara was so caught up in her own grief she didn't hear the truck coming up the drive.

Strong, muscular arms scooped her up from the ground, pulling her onto hard, muscular thighs. Tara knew by his scent that Johnny held her in his arms, cradling her on his lap. He rocked her and ran a large palm up and down her back, trying to soothe her pain away. He had always been the more sensitive, compassionate one out of him and Clay. Tara clutched his shirt in her hands as she cried. He didn't try to stop her, just held and rocked her. When she finally stopped, she slumped against his chest, savoring the comfort and touch of another human being. Before today, it had been so long since she had been held and comforted. She never wanted to let go.

"Are you all right, sweetheart?" Johnny asked as he tipped her head up to his with a finger beneath her chin.

Tara nodded then shook her head. She wasn't all right and didn't know if she ever would be again.

"Talk to me, Tara."

"I can't do this anymore, Johnny," Tara replied with a sob.

"What can't you do, sweetheart?"

"I'm so lonely. My mom died over six years ago. My dad left years ago. I have no friends. I can't do this anymore."

"Tara, don't talk like that. You have me and Clay. We'll always be here for you, sweetheart," Johnny replied, and Tara could see anguish on his face for her as she spoke, but she didn't trust him or Clay anymore and didn't know if she ever would. She was still that little girl inside. She knew she still loved Johnny and Clay but didn't think she would ever have that trust again.

"No. I don't have you and Clay. I never have," Tara responded, pushing up and off Johnny's lap.

"What the fuck are you talking about, Tara?" Johnny said as he stood and walked over to her. He grasped her by her upper arms so she couldn't escape him.

"You and Clay tolerated me as a kid. You didn't really want me around or like me. If you had, I never would have found you in the barn fucking that woman," Tara yelled as she glared at Johnny.

"Now, that's where you're wrong, little girl. We were a lot older than you and had needs. We wanted you, but we couldn't do anything about it. What do you think would have happened if we had made a move on you and someone had found out? We would have ended up in jail, for God's sakes. But there is nothing stopping us from doing anything now," Johnny stated. He pulled her in closer to him and placed his mouth down over hers.

Tara whimpered as Johnny leaned down to her and slanted his

mouth, sliding his lips over hers. She heard him groan as his mouth touched hers for the first time. The first taste of him exploded on her taste buds as he slid his tongue in between her lips and teeth, sliding his alongside hers. He grasped her hips and pulled her firmly against his body, thrusting his hips into her stomach as he devoured her mouth. He palmed the back of her head, keeping her in place so she couldn't pull away. She felt his cock jerking against the zipper of his jeans as he pushed his hips into hers. To have him kissing and grinding his cock against her nearly had her coming in her pants. Johnny couldn't seem to get enough of her. The taste of his mouth and tongue, as well as the feel of his warm, hard body pressed up against her own soft form was absolute heaven. She wanted him to bury his cock in her achy, wet pussy right now. She moaned with unrequited desire as he pulled his mouth from hers, resting his forehead against her own as they panted for breath and stared into each other's passion-glazed eyes.

"I want you, Tara. We both want you. You are not leaving here again. We're not going to let you. And if I ever hear you talk the way you did before, I'll put you over my knee and spank your ass till its pink. Do you understand?" Johnny growled.

Tara took a step back from Johnny, watching him warily, her breathing fast. She couldn't believe he had just kissed her, told her that he and Clay wanted her. She didn't know if she believed him or if she was just another conquest. Another notch on their bedpost. Her emotions were in turmoil, and she couldn't have answered him if her life depended on it. She wrapped her arms around her body protectively and turned her back to him. She stood leaning against the corral fence as she stared into the distance.

Whack. Tara jumped and spun around to stare at Johnny, her eyes wide in disbelief that he had just spanked her on the ass.

"I asked you a question, Tara. Don't you ever turn your back on me again. Now answer me, or I will put you over my knee right here, right now. I will bare your ass and paddle you good, and I don't care who sees."

"Yes. I understand," Tara replied in a husky, quiet voice.

"Good. Now, what the hell are you doing out here? You're supposed to be resting," Johnny stated with narrowed eyes.

"I needed some fresh air. I feel fine, and I haven't done anything. I have had just about as much rest as I can stand. I was beginning to get cabin fever," Tara replied, thrusting her chin at Johnny defiantly.

Tara and Johnny turned at the sound of pounding horse hooves. Clay was heading their way. Tara didn't think she was up to dealing with Clay after her altercation with Johnny. Johnny had shocked her. He had always been so easygoing. He was always smiling, friendly, and such a flirt. Tara had never seen the dominant side of Johnny before. Clay was the more serious of the two brothers. He had always laid down the law and kept her in line. He still smiled a lot, but with Clay she never knew when she had pushed too far until he hauled back on the ropes to rein her in. But rules were rules, and she'd better look out if she broke any of Clay's rules.

Tara turned away from Clay and Johnny, intending to get back to the house and her room. She'd had more than enough of them for one day. She was halfway across the yard when the pounding hooves sped up. Tara knew without looking Clay was heading in her direction. She picked up her pace, hoping to make it to the house steps and avoid another confrontation.

She wasn't fast enough. She gave a squeak of fright as the ground beneath her feet trembled with vibrations as Clay and his mount drew near. She gave up any pretense and broke into a run. The next thing she knew, a band of steel had wrapped around her waist and she was flying through the air. She landed on Clay's hard, muscular thighs, which stopped her screech of fear and fury. Clay slowed the horse to a trot and then turned his mount back to where Johnny was standing.

Tara took in Johnny's aggressive stance. His hips were thrust forward, his legs were spread shoulder width apart, and his arms were crossed over his muscular chest. The scowl on his face told her she was in deep shit.

Tara averted her eyes then made the mistake of looking up at Clay. He was staring down at her, and the heat, the hunger, evident in his eyes was enough to set her on fire. She tried to push his large, muscular arm away from around her waist, but gave up the futile effort. She was not getting away from him until he released her.

Clay lifted Tara up into his arms and dismounted from his horse, leaving her in the saddle as he kept his eyes on her. He grasped her about the waist and pulled her from his horse, holding her at eye level with her feet dangling in the air.

"Brandon, come and get Thunder. I want you to cool him off, give him a rub down and some feed," Clay commanded as his ranch hand appeared.

"Sure thing, boss."

Tara felt her cheeks pinken with the knowledge Brandon could see the way Clay held her off the ground with ease.

"Please put me down, Clay."

"No," Clay replied.

Tara's world spun so fast her vision blurred. She was hanging upside down over Clay's hard, muscular shoulder, her head hanging down to his lower back. He had an arm wrapped around her knees, and a large hand was spread over the cheeks of her ass. He turned around and headed for the house and didn't stop until he gently placed her on the bed.

"As much as I like you wearing my clothes, baby, get them off. Now," Clay demanded forcefully.

"What? What for?"

"I'm at the end of my tether, Tara. Get. Your. Clothes. Off. Now."

Tara moved fast, surprising herself at her own speed and agility. She was off the bed and standing on the other side before Clay had a chance to stop her. The look he gave her was so predatory she could feel her heart racing. Johnny entered the bedroom and stood with his hips thrust forward in an impressive display of dominance. Tara stepped back and knew she was in trouble, cornered, trapped, when her back hit the wall.

"I found Tara sitting on the ground when I got back from town bawling her eyes out. Do you want to know what she said?" Johnny asked Clay without taking his eyes from her.

"Tell me," Clay replied.

"She said she can't do this anymore. She's sick of being lonely and alone. She said she has no friends, not even us. She said she never had us because she found us in the barn fucking that woman the day she was leaving town."

"What? Is that what you think, Tara?" Clay asked, moving toward the end of the bed.

Tara couldn't answer Clay. She stood in shock as the two men she had grown up with looked at her with hunger in their eyes. She pushed herself back into the corner of the room. Her heart was beating a rapid staccato as she panted air in and out of her lungs quickly. She licked her dry lips, keeping her eyes on the two men moving forward with slow, measured steps.

"Answer me, now. Or I swear to God I will strip you naked, put you over my knee, and paddle your ass," Clay bit out between clenched teeth.

Hearing the words she just said coming out of Johnny's mouth gave Tara pause. She had never been a quitter, and she could tell by the looks on Clay's and Johnny's faces she had scared them with her words. She wanted to explain how she felt at the time she'd spouted those words, but she didn't know if they would believe her.

Tara was too afraid to answer. She didn't want to be distracted. She felt her pussy clench with need. Excitement permeated her body, making her nipples pucker and thrust against the fabric of the shirt. For the first time in six years, she felt alive again. She wanted to smile, but bit the inside of her cheek to prevent herself from doing so. Clay would see her smile as a taunt, a challenge, and she knew he wouldn't back down. He never had. But she had waited for this moment for years, and there was no way in hell she was letting it pass. So she decided to goad Clay into giving her what she wanted.

"Game on!" Tara stated firmly.

"Oh, you are in so much trouble, baby. You know the rules. When I ask you a question or tell you to do something, you obey. I am going to tan your ass good, but this time I'm not doing it through your clothes. I am going to strip you naked. Your ass is going to be bright pink by the time I finish with you," Clay stated.

They were moving in on her, and Tara only had one way to go. Up and over the bed. She moved quickly, jumped onto the bed, and gave a scream of frustration as one of her ankles was grasped by a large hand. She went down with a screech of fury and tried to kick whoever had a hold of her. A large body landed on top her, pinning her to the bed. There was no way she could get out of this now. Her pussy ached and spasmed with need. The thought of her two men finally loving her was nearly more than she could stand. She couldn't wait to feel their hands and mouths on her body. Tara had always wanted to be dominated. She had dreamed of Clay and Johnny taking over control in the bedroom. She felt a thrill of excitement course through her body. Her muscles softened, and her pussy clenched with unrequited desire. She could feel copious amounts of juices leaking out of her sex and couldn't prevent a whimper of arousal from escaping her mouth. She looked up into Clay's heated eyes and knew by the look on his face her gaze mirrored his.

Chapter Six

"Johnny, go get the restraints," Clay growled as he pinned Tara to the bed with his body. She was trying to buck him off, and he smiled to himself. He knew she didn't have a chance in hell of escaping them. He made sure some of his weight was resting on his arms and legs so he wouldn't crush their woman. The last thing he wanted to do was hurt her.

"I want this, but get the fuck off me," Tara yelled at Clay as she kicked and bucked, trying to escape. But Clay knew she was only toying with him. There was no fear or demand, no emphasis to her words, and he knew she was testing him and Johnny. She wanted him and his brother to prove to her that they could earn her respect and be the men she needed them to be.

"Oh, you are so going to get it, baby. I am going to smack your ass good," Clay breathed against Tara's ear. He gave a chuckle when he felt her shiver beneath him and her halfhearted struggles stopped. Instead she arched up into his body. His little woman was getting turned on. He couldn't wait to strip her naked and pleasure her. He and Johnny had waited far too long already, and they weren't going to hold back anymore.

Johnny grasped one of Tara's arms, straightened it out above her head, tied the soft fabric around her wrist, and threaded the end of the thin restraint through the rings attached to the headboard. He then repeated the process with her other arm until she was bound and couldn't move her arms more than a couple of inches. The great thing about the restraints was that they were soft and flexible, so they could flip her over as many times as they liked and know they wouldn't hurt her.

Clay eased his way down Tara's slim body, keeping a hand in the middle of her back so she couldn't move too much. He knelt between her legs and motioned Johnny over to help him strip her clothes off. Clay turned Tara over, took in the sight of her flushed face and the rapidly beating pulse at the base of her throat. Her eyes were dilated and had a glassy sheen over them. His little baby was aroused.

Clay undid his borrowed belt and pulled it apart from around her waist. Next he flicked the button of his jeans his woman was wearing and eased the zipper down. He pulled until he had them and her panties around her knees. Tara was now lying quietly on the bed, her heated stare watching everything he and his brother were doing to her. He moved down to her feet and pulled the clothes off over her feet.

Clay watched as Johnny moved up to the bedside, knelt above Tara, and stared into her eyes as he gripped the neck of the T-shirt she was wearing. He smiled as his brother ripped the shirt from top to bottom and spread the sides out, revealing her delectable little body.

Clay picked up the other restraints on the bed, flipped Tara back over to her stomach, grasped an ankle in his large hand, and pulled her leg wide. He bound her leg with the soft material and hooked it over the rail at the foot of the bed. He repeated the process until her legs were spread wide across the mattress.

Johnny released one of her hands from the restraint, pulled her borrowed jacket and shirt down off one arm, then tethered her once more and did the same to her other arm. He grabbed a pillow from the top of the bed, moved down her side, lifted her hips, and shoved the pillow beneath her. They had her in the perfect position for a spanking.

"Let me the fuck go now. I hate you two," Tara yelled at them, but then contradicted her words by pushing her hips up toward them, begging for more of their touch.

"Oh, no you don't, sweetheart. You don't hate us at all, because if you did, you wouldn't be lying there panting with need or bucking up, begging for our touch. But you're not really upset. I can see your eyes begging us to touch you," Johnny replied with a chuckle.

Tara didn't bother to reply. She closed her eyes and sighed, letting Clay know she had been waiting for this moment. He intended to make sure she enjoyed every minute of his and his brother's dominance.

Whack.

"Ow, that hurt."

"It was supposed to, baby. You know the rules. You have known our rules since you were a kid. You're not allowed to swear, and you didn't answer when I asked you a question. Not to mention what you said to Johnny earlier. So far you have racked up three punishments, and that's being lenient. Keep cussing and I'll add more," Clay said, smoothing a hand over her warm, silky ass.

Whack. Whack. Whack.

"Hmm, I love to see your ass a nice pretty pink color. It gets me so hard I could pound nails," Johnny whispered in Tara's ear, but loud enough for Clay to hear.

Clay smoothed his hand over Tara's hot bottom. He gave a chuckle as she thrust her hips up into his hand. He grasped the fleshy globes of her ass, massaging the lush pink flesh, being careful not to hurt her.

"You like getting your ass spanked, don't ya, baby?" Clay asked.

"No."

Whack. "Don't lie to me, Tara. I'll bet if I touch your pussy, I'm gonna find it nice and wet. Won't I, baby?"

"No," Tara lied as she gasped with pleasure.

Whack. "Let's find out. If you're all creamy and wet, I'm gonna spank you some more for lying to me, Tara."

Clay slid his hands down over Tara's buttocks and down the back of her thighs. He then put his large hands on the inside of her thighs and slowly ran his hands up her warm legs. He dipped one finger into the warm, wet well and had to bite his tongue at the pool of moisture he found. Their little baby was dripping.

"Oh, you are in so much trouble," Clay said and punctuated his statement with the palm of his hand. "You lied to me, Tara." *Whack.* "That's seven, baby."

Clay slid down between Tara's legs until his face was level with her creamy cunt. He placed his arms over and around her thighs and lifted her ass a little higher into the air. He bent down and inhaled the delicious scent of aroused woman. He slid his tongue out between the folds of her creamy sex, groaning at the ambrosia coating his tongue. He couldn't get enough of her. He opened his mouth wide and devoured her pussy, holding Tara in place as she wriggled and squirmed beneath his mouth.

Clay laved his tongue over and around her delicate folds of flesh, flicking across her engorged clit every few strokes until he had Tara pushing her hips up into his mouth. He slid down through her folds and speared his tongue into her wet little hole, growling with satisfaction when he felt her muscles clench and release around his slick muscle. He moved back up, flattened his tongue, twirling and sliding it across her nub. He moved one of his arms and slid the tip of a large, thick finger just inside her tight hole.

"Oh my God. What are you doing to me?" Tara moaned, thrusting her hips at Clay.

"Clay's punishing you, sweetheart. He is going to take you to the brink of orgasm again and again, but he's not gonna let you go over," Johnny whispered into Tara's ear.

* * * *

Tara felt Johnny turn her face to him with a gentle finger beneath her chin, and then he slanted his mouth over hers. The feel of him thrusting his tongue in and out of her mouth, mimicking the sex act, copying the shallow thrusts of Clay's finger in and out of her pussy, had her mewing in the back of her throat. He pushed a hand underneath her body, sought out one of her plump mounds, and tweaked her nipple between a finger and thumb until it was hard. He flicked his thumb over the peak, heightening her senses, as pleasure shot from her nipple down through her body to her throbbing clit. She couldn't believe the sounds she made as they pleasured her. She would never have guessed she was capable of such animalistic noises.

The feel of Clay sliding more of his finger into her dripping sex and growling around her clit as her muscles fluttered along the length of his finger had her on the brink of orgasm. He pushed more and more of his digit into her sheath until she felt a slight pain as he encountered the thin membrane of skin protecting her womb. She felt him remove his mouth from her mound and turned her head in time to see him grabbing at his balls through his jeans. Obviously he was on the brink as well and had stopped his cock from shooting off. She moaned as he withdrew his finger from her cunt, rose from the bed, and began to remove his clothes.

"Johnny, turn her over. Tara, are you a virgin, baby?" Clay asked, his voice deep and husky with passion.

Tara knew Clay must have felt how tight she was, and the sight of his possessive stare heated her blood even more. But she'd be damned if she would admit to having no experience. He or Johnny would find out soon enough anyway, once one of them put her out of her sexual misery and stuffed her full of cock.

"No. Of course I'm not. What makes you think I would still be a virgin at my age?" Tara spat out as she glared at Clay after Johnny had turned her over to lie on her back. She was grateful she didn't have to crick her neck to look at them anymore. Tara was surprised she didn't feel the restraints around her ankles and wrists tighten. She looked above her head and saw the restraints were attached to small rings on the rails of the headboard, which would swivel around every time they turned her. Tara gasped as she looked back at Clay to see him standing totally naked as he looked at her. He was so broad and muscular.

Tara perused his body from the top of his black collar-length hair, over his broad forehead, his bright-green eyes, wide, muscular shoulders, and broad chest, down over his washboard abs and narrow hips, down the length of his long, muscular legs, then snapped her gaze back to the large appendage between his legs. The man was hung. His cock was jutting out from his groin, bobbing up and down with the beat of his heart. He was wide and long, the head of his cock an angry purple color. Tara's breath rasped in and out of her lungs with excitement and trepidation. There was no way he was going to fit that monster in her body.

Tara watched as Clay took a step toward her then climbed onto the bed. He crawled up between her legs and sat back on his haunches. He leaned forward, grasped Tara's chin between his thumb and finger, pinning her with his eyes.

"I'm going to ask you one more time, baby, and if you don't answer me with the truth I'm going to spank you, again. Have you ever had sex, Tara?" Clay asked.

Tara hesitated. She didn't want him to know she was still a virgin, that she hadn't found anyone to share her body with, but if she lied, she could end up getting spanked. Even though she would enjoy the spanking, she didn't want to lie about her inexperience. She knew he and Johnny would be able to tell if she fibbed.

"No," Tara whispered.

"I couldn't hear you, baby. Tell me again, louder this time," Clay commanded.

"No," Tara screamed at him. "Are you happy now that you've humiliated me?"

"My intention is not to hurt you, Tara, not to humiliate you. You have nothing to be ashamed of, Tara. You should be proud of the fact you're still a virgin. I'm glad you haven't shared your body with anyone, 'cos once we have taken you, you'll belong to us. No one else is going to touch you. You belong to me and Johnny. My God, what do you think would have happened to you if I had believed your lie and thrust into your body without being gentle? I would have hurt you badly. You are a very naughty girl," Clay said then smacked his hand down onto her pussy.

Tara screamed, and then the scream turned to a moan as she thrust her hips up at him. She couldn't believe Clay had just spanked her pussy, but she wanted him to do it again. She couldn't believe the heat from the sting turned into pleasure, making her pussy tingle and weep.

"You liked that didn't you, sweetheart? I can't wait until Clay is buried in your tight little cunt. Then I am going to fuck that sweet, lush ass. We are going to give you so much pleasure, you're going to be begging us to fuck you," Tara heard Johnny whisper in her ear.

Tara could see Clay and Johnny watching her as she rode the sensations of pain turning to pleasure. She could tell he was taking things slow with her and still would as he penetrated her body for the first time, but she knew she had no control over what they were going to do to her. Not that she wanted to. She'd dreamed of this moment for years, and there was no way she was going to spoil things by playing too hard to get. She knew she still had to follow their rules. Clay and his brother were dominant in bed. She'd seen that for her own eyes when she had caught them fucking that woman years ago and knew they weren't going to make any exceptions for her. She could see they needed her to know they were the ones in control in the bedroom as well as out of it.

"I don't belong to anyone, you bastard," Tara yelled at Clay, goading him with her mouth. She would love to see such a controlled man lose control of himself and give her what she wanted—his cock shoved into the depths of her pussy.

"Oh, that's where you're wrong, baby. You belong to us now, and we're not letting you go. Johnny, go and get the scissors, shaving cream, razor, and a bowl of warm water," Clay commanded.

Tara didn't want to seem to give in too easily, but her limbs were getting tired of struggling, and she had to settle down to gather some stamina to fight them more. She was turning herself on by fighting them and knew by the look on Clay's and Johnny's faces they were just as aroused.

She couldn't believe Clay had already brought her close to orgasm twice, or how turned on she was by fighting them. She couldn't wait for the real games to begin. Tara saw Johnny reenter the bedroom once more with a bowl full of water, a small pair of scissors in his hand, as well as a razor and a can of shaving cream. He placed them on the side of the bed, put the bowl of water on the floor, then pulled a towel out from beneath his arm. He lifted Tara's hips up as Clay removed the pillow and replaced it with the towel.

"What the fuck do you think you are doing? What if I don't want my pussy shaved?" Tara yelled as she glared at Clay then Johnny.

"When it comes to the bedroom, you will do as we say, Tara," Clay stated.

Tara saw Clay reach for the pair of scissors and begin clipping her pubic hair. Once he had it shorter all over, he lathered her pussy with shaving cream then began to shave her pubic hair off. When that was done, he grabbed a washcloth from the bowl, wrung it out, then wiped the remnants of shaving cream from her mound. He removed the towel from beneath her hips and watched Johnny move everything out of the way.

Tara saw Clay move back down between her legs until he was lying on his stomach, his head level with her pussy. She felt him blow gently over her exposed flesh and saw his smug satisfaction as her pussy clenched and released. Tara couldn't help the sound she made deep in her chest as he bent his head down and took one long lick from her wet hole up to her clit. His groan joined hers as his tongue elicited a sharp, pulsing need deep in her womb. She wanted him to bury himself in her body right then, but knew he needed to show her she wasn't the one in control, and she loved every minute of it. Clay had already told her their rules were to be obeyed, and she couldn't wait for the two punishments he advised she had racked up.

Tara moaned and bucked her hips as Clay devoured her pussy, sliding his tongue up and down through her moisture-coated folds.

She felt him push a fingertip into her body while laving her clit, enhancing her pleasure. Tara saw Clay open his eyes and watch his brother as Johnny lowered his head and began sucking one of her hard nipples into his mouth, whilst he pinched and flicked her other nipple.

Tara was on fire. She couldn't contain her sounds of arousal any longer, and she thrust her breasts and hips up, demanding more pleasure. She cried out as Clay pushed his finger into her tight, wet sheath until it was buried to the second knuckle. She felt him twist it around inside her body and begin to rub over a sensitive spongy spot deep inside. She'd heard about a female's G-spot and was ecstatic that Clay had found hers with ease. In a matter of seconds her body was making lewd squelching sounds, and the spongy area inside her expanded toward his finger. She whimpered as Clay rubbed faster over her sweet spot until she was on the brink of climax. She could feel her pussy walls fluttering around his digit, trying to draw him in deeper. She was shocked when he withdrew his finger and mouth from her sex and then watched as Johnny withdrew from her breasts.

Tara screamed and sobbed with frustration. She had been so close, and to have them stop was pure torture, but she knew her men were the ones in control. They were trying to teach her that it was their way in the bedroom as she was to abide by their rules. And she loved every minute of it.

"Do you know how sexy you are, Tara? My God, if you could see yourself the way we do right now. Your face is flushed, your nipples are hard, begging for attention, and this little bald pussy is bright pink. Your clit is protruding, just begging for our touch," Clay advised in a deep, husky voice. "You have one more punishment left, then we are going to fuck you and send you flying. I can't wait to have your sweet cunt wrapped around my cock, squeezing and milking the cum from my balls."

"Please let me go and fuck me," Tara sobbed, tears leaking from the corner of her eyes, desperate to reach climax. "I can't do this anymore. I need to come."

"I'll let you out of the bindings, sweetheart, but we're never letting you go. You're ours, Tara, and the sooner you come to terms with that, the better off we'll all be," Johnny said in a quiet voice, full of compassion, as he released her from the restraints.

Tara reached out and pulled him to her, wrapping her arms around his neck and sighing with bliss as his body came in contact with her naked breasts.

Tara saw Clay bend his head back down to her pussy and begin the process of punishing her one last time. She could tell the punishments he and Johnny were giving her were a lot harder on them than they were on her. The skin on their faces was drawn tight, sweat had gathered on their foreheads, and she could see both of their hands shaking At least she was experiencing the touch of their mouths and hands on her body, as well as the pleasure they were inflicting on her. Clay and Johnny had to hold off from what she could see they really wanted to do. She could tell by the longing on their faces and knew they wanted to bury themselves in her body the moment they had seen her naked and spread out before them on the bed. She knew their self-control was being tested to the limit.

Tara groaned as Clay eased his finger inside her wet pussy while he laved his tongue over her engorged clit. Her muscles clamped down around his finger as he slid his digit over her G-spot once more. He flicked his tongue over her clit rapidly, repeatedly, until he had her hips bowed up off the bed. She felt him gently grasp her sensitive nub between his lips and suck firmly as he rubbed the pad of his finger on her sweet spot. She clamped down on his finger hard as he sent her over the edge into ecstasy for the first time. She screamed and bucked, her body shaking uncontrollably, and felt her pussy gush her juices and knew she had covered his hand.

Chapter Seven

Tara felt as if she was totally wrung out after Johnny and Clay had delivered her punishments. She gave a sigh and closed her eyes. She felt as if she were floating on a cloud. She had never been so relaxed or satiated in her life. She wanted to curl up and go to sleep.

She felt Clay move up between her legs, and then she gave a groan as she felt him sliding the head of his cock along her slick, wet folds. She didn't think she could handle any more of their attention. She gasped as she felt her folds stretch to accommodate Clay's wide cock, the burning pain turning to pleasure as he popped through her tight flesh.

"Oh yeah, baby. Your little cunt feels so good wrapped around my cock. Can you feel your pussy trying to pull me in? You're incredible, Tara," Clay rasped out as he pushed a little more of his cock into her body.

Tara could see sweat rolling down over Clay's face as he held still, giving Tara's body time to adjust to his penetration. The feel of his cock sliding back a little then pushing forward another inch was pure heaven. She felt him wrap the palm of his hand around his balls and pulled down firmly to prevent his cock shooting off too early, but she wanted him buried in her now. She wanted to feel his cock sliding in and out of her wet pussy and then to feel him bury himself into her body balls-deep as she felt her cunt ripple and clench around his rod, to feel herself climax around his hard flesh as she milked the cum from his balls, as he shot off deep inside her.

She felt him slide back in again and push into her another couple of inches. They groaned together as their flesh pulsed, the sensations making her want to thrust her hips up into his and feel his cock to the hilt in her body. Much to Tara's frustration, he held still as she felt the tip of his rod pushing against her tight flesh. She could feel a slight pinch as his cock stretched her virgin flesh. He held tightly onto her hips to control her movements, but she wanted to impale herself on his cock, to feel his hard rod stretching and filling her to capacity.

"Clay. Oh God. What are you doing to me? Please," Tara cried.

"Please what, baby?"

"Please, fuck me," Tara yelled as she tried to wiggle her hips.

"Tara, hold still. You need to let Clay set the pace, sweetheart. If you go too hard too fast, you'll end up hurting yourself," Johnny stated off to her side.

Tara turned her head to see Johnny climbing on the bed totally naked. She hadn't even been aware he had moved to remove his clothes. He was built like his brother, only there was more of him. He had more muscles than Clay, was a few inches taller, and his cock looked to be longer, but just as wide as his brother's. His dark-brown hair flopped over his forehead, and his hazel eyes pinned her to the spot when she moved her gaze back to his.

"I can't wait anymore, Tara. I need that sweet mouth on my cock. Open up, sweetheart," Johnny commanded as he ran the tip of his cock over her full lower lip.

Tara slid her tongue from her mouth and ran it over the small hole of Johnny's cock. The salty, spicy flavor of his pre-cum had her wanting to devour him. She licked around the head of his rod and gave a growl of approval at his groan.

"Oh yeah. That's it, Tara, get me nice and wet so you can suck me down. Your mouth feels so good."

Johnny's explicit words turned Tara on even more. She opened her mouth wide and sucked him into her mouth as she tried to buck her hips, hoping to get Clay to move in her pussy.

"Tara, you look so good sucking Johnny's cock. Do you like sucking cock, baby?" Clay asked as he withdrew his penis a little from her tight snatch.

Tara groaned as she sucked more of Johnny into her mouth. She swirled her tongue on the sensitive underside of his cock, then sucked him in as far as she could handle without gagging. She set up a slow bobbing rhythm, gliding up and down his cock, using the muscles in her mouth to suck firmly on her up slide. Clay was thrusting his hips, sliding his hard flesh in and out of her vagina, his cock making shallow slides into her body. She wanted him to bury himself all the way inside of her.

She felt Johnny grab a handful of her hair and hold her head still as he began to thrust his hips in a slow, easy rhythm in and out of her mouth. The feel of his cock sliding in and retreating along her tongue, and the sensation of her lips wrapped around his cock were driving her to distraction. The sound of him grinding his teeth made her realize she was giving him so much pleasure that he was on the brink of control. She saw his hand disappear then felt it brush her chin, and he clasped his balls to prevent from climaxing too soon. It was a heady feeling to know she turned him on so much.

Tara felt Clay's cock hit a particularly tight spot inside her body. She felt the skin stretch, and the slight sting of pain had her flinching and groaning around Johnny's cock. He must have liked that because he moaned and thrust into her mouth a little further. Clay slid back and pushed into her again and again. She felt the muscles of her pussy ripple along the length of his hard flesh.

"Johnny, help her over," Clay rasped out.

She saw Johnny lean over her body, still maintaining his rhythm of advance and retreat in her mouth, and then he slid a hand to the top of her slit. He began to massage her clit with the pad of a finger and was rewarded with another one of her moans.

Tara moaned with pleasure as Clay slid back again, grasped her hips more firmly as her walls clamped down on his buried flesh, and thrust through her virgin barrier. He held still as her flesh massaged his cock, gave a growl, and she knew he was close to climaxing. She could feel his impaled flesh pulsing inside of her. She felt him pull back out and thrust in again. Once, twice, three more times, he thrust into her clenching flesh and gave a roar as her rippling, clenching sheath milked the cum from his balls. His pulsing flesh sent her over the edge again, his climax enhancing her pleasure.

"Tara, I'm gonna come, sweetheart. If you don't want my cum in your mouth, pull off now," Johnny panted out.

Tara knew she surprised Johnny by sucking his cock into her mouth until he hit the back of her throat when his eyes widened. She retreated to swirl her tongue on the sensitive bundle of nerves beneath the crown of his cock, then suctioned him into her depths once more. The sound of Johnny's roar made Tara feel so powerful as his cock pulsed in her mouth and shot his cum over her tongue and down the back of her throat. For the first time in her life, she felt what it was like to be feminine and in control of someone else's pleasure. It was a heady feeling.

Tara wrapped her arms and legs around Clay when he slumped down on top of her. She could feel his limbs shaking and knew he felt as weak as she did, as weak as a newborn foal. Tara was appreciative when he made sure to keep his body off of her by using his elbows to hold some of his weight, so he wouldn't crush her. She looked up to see him watching as Johnny slowly pulled his deflating cock from Tara's mouth. She heard his sigh of satisfaction as her mouth made a popping sound as he kissed her shoulder.

Tara could see the experience of making love with her had shaken Clay. She knew they had just set out to dominate and punish her, and she had turned to tables on them by giving over the control of her body and its responses to Clay and Johnny. She was the one who had controlled them in the end. She had made them both lose control and knew she wanted to experience that again and again. It was a heady, powerful feeling. It had her confidence returning, and she knew no matter how much they dominated her, held her down, and pleasured her, she was the one in control of all their pleasure.

Tara heard Clay's breathing finally slow and noticed his limbs had stopped shaking. She stared into his eyes as he pushed himself up further on his arms so he was once more on his knees between her legs. She saw his gaze move to his brother and knew he was watching Johnny massage her arms and legs, helping to ease her back down from her climactic high. Tara moaned and closed her eyes again. She gave a sigh then curled up on her side, fighting sleep, content at being in their home and at finally having her two men love her with their bodies. She felt Clay curl up at her back, and Johnny climbed into bed, pushing his back up against her front. She wrapped an arm around Johnny's waist, breathed in his masculine scent, and drifted into sleep.

Chapter Eight

Tara took a long, hot shower, relishing the feel of the water on her sore body. She washed her hair and skin then stepped out. Tara stretched and groaned as her sore muscles protested, as well as the sensitive flesh between her thighs, and slipped into the bath she readied earlier. She savored the warm water she was now soaking in, her muscles easing as the water penetrated to her bones. Once done, she dried off and exited.

Tara walked into the bedroom, a large bath towel wrapped around her breasts and ending just below her knees, and stopped as she saw Johnny enter the room with shopping bags in his hands. She watched him as he placed the bags on the bed, walked up to her, tilted her face to his with a finger beneath her chin, and kissed her. He had embers firing her body up as he plundered her mouth with his lips and tongue. He drew back from her after she had slumped against his chest, holding her upper arms to steady her as she looked up into his face.

"How are you feeling, sweetheart?"

"Sore," Tara blurted then lowered her eyes as she felt her cheeks flush with heat.

"You have nothing to be embarrassed about, Tara. You're such a sexy little thing," Johnny stated then gave a bark of laughter, and she knew he had noticed her cheeks flushing red. "I bought you some clothes, honey. Why don't you get dressed? When you're done, come into the kitchen. I've just made a fresh pot of coffee."

"Where's Clay?"

"He's out in the barn. He'll be back soon. Hurry up, sweetheart," Johnny commanded, turned her around by her shoulders, and then popped her ass before he walked out the door.

Tara sighed as she watched his denim-covered ass until he was no longer in sight. Her heart was so full of love for Johnny and Clay. She had loved them for such a long time. She wanted nothing more than to tell them she loved them, but didn't want to say those three words for the first time. Not until she was sure they loved her, too. Sure they said they wanted her, had wanted her since she was a teenager, but wanting and needing were vastly different from loving. There was no way she was putting herself, her pride, on the line before she knew for sure her love was returned. She knew she was setting herself up for another fall, but where those two men were concerned, she couldn't seem to help herself.

Tara pulled out some sexy underwear Johnny had purchased from a lingerie shop, found some jeans and a T-shirt. She pulled on the new clothes and then put the rest of the clothes away. It looked like he had bought her enough to last an entire week without her having to do any washing. She was going to be paying off her debt for the next month at least. Johnny hadn't left any of the price tags on the clothes, so she was only guessing at the amount she now owed him and Clay. There wasn't much she could do about it just now. She didn't have any of her bank or credit cards, and what little money she had saved would be gone when she paid them back, if it was even enough to cover the cost of the clothes. Tara pushed her thoughts to the back of her mind and left the bedroom. The smell of coffee was tempting her, so she followed her nose.

Tara sat down at the dining table and sipped from her coffee mug, aware of Johnny's eyes on her the whole time. She didn't know what they wanted from her. She wasn't good with people anymore. Not since her and her mother had left Slick Rock. They had both been too busy going to school and working. She and her mom hadn't done any socializing. They spent day in, day out, week after week, year after year, just trying to survive. The two years she and her mom had spent together in Denver had been one big struggle. It had continued to be more of a struggle when Tara's mom had died. Tara had closed herself off from everyone. She had been numb with grief and so alone she had been afraid to let herself feel.

Johnny and Clay were forcing her back into the land of the living. The pain of it was too intense for her to endure. She needed to grasp that numbness, build the walls around her heart, bigger and stronger than ever before. Otherwise they would end up destroying her. She needed to find another job, a place to live, so she could go back to existing.

Tara moved on her chair, her sore muscles reminding her of their previous night's activities. They had seduced her so effectively. She hadn't been able to resist them once they had stripped her naked and touched her body, not that she had really wanted to. Her body, mind, and heart were screaming out for the touch of another human being. But if she allowed that again, she was scared she would shatter into a million pieces. Tara knew the only way to keep her heart safe was to leave. She had to figure out a way to get away from two of the people she loved most in the world besides her mom. Johnny came to the table and sat down beside her.

"Tara, talk to me, sweetheart. I can see the pain in your eyes. Tell me what's going on with you. Please?"

"I'm fine. Just a little tired, I guess."

"Don't you dare fucking lie to me, Tara. Talk to me. I'm trying to help you," Johnny reiterated.

"What the hell do you want from me? You and your brother have taken my body. I have nothing left. Don't you understand? You've had all there is to have of me," Tara screamed at Johnny as she rose from her seat and ran out the back door. She was blinded by tears and ran smack into a hard, large, immovable object.

Clay wrapped his arms around Tara to prevent her from falling backward. He swung her up into his arms and held her against his chest.

"Leave me alone. Put me, the fuck, down," Tara yelled then

contradicted her own words by clinging to him. "Hold me. God, please just hold me."

Clay didn't respond as she beat her small hands against his shoulders and chest. He held her in his strong arms and entered the house just as Johnny was about to exit. His brother held the door open for him, and he strode to the living room, sank down onto the large sofa with Tara still in his arms. He let her ass slide down onto his lap and held her immobile with arms banded around her arms and chest, effectively trapping her.

Tara didn't quit fighting Clay's hold until she had totally exhausted herself. She knew she had been fighting a losing battle, but she had to try anyway. She didn't want to feel any more pain, but they were determined to bring her back into the land of the living. She wished she still couldn't remember anything before the day she had found herself in the diner in Slick Rock with Johnny and Clay looking at her with concern. Life would be so much easier. But she wasn't a quitter. She never had been. She was going to have to face up to reality, and it looked like Clay and Johnny weren't going to let her hide the way she wanted to right now.

Tara had fought for everything in her life. Every step had been a struggle since before, and even more so after, she had left her childhood home of Slick Rock. She wasn't one to give up without a fight. She was just like her mom. When they decided to do something, they did it, or at least worked toward it to make it happen. The loss of her mom had been so hard on her. Then the loss of her home had been the clincher. She had never thought she would be the type of person to give up. She was just too tired and overwhelmed at the moment to think clearly. Clay and Johnny weren't going to let her hide, as much as she wanted to. They were forcing her to feel, and she was beginning to feel way too much.

"Tara, look at me," Clay commanded.

Tara tried to ignore his command but soon found her eyes drawn to him.

"We are trying to help you, baby. You need to talk to us. Tell us why you are in so much pain. We can see it in your eyes," Clay stated with compassion.

"If you want to help me, then let me go," Tara wailed, holding on to her composure by a thread.

"No. We're never letting you go again, baby. You belong to us," Clay stated in a firm voice.

"I'm not a fucking possession. I don't belong to anyone. I'm my own person. Can't you see that? I don't belong anywhere," Tara screamed as the dam broke.

Once Tara started crying she couldn't stop. She sobbed and cried until she could hardly breathe. She had spent the last six years alone, pushing the grief of losing her mom to the back of her mind. But the last eight years, her heart had been so shattered she didn't think she would ever be able to put it back together. She felt as if she would never be whole again. Everyone she ever loved left her. First her father had left her and her mom, then she had walked into the barn to find the loves of her life with another woman, and then her mom had died. She had no one and nothing left.

* * * *

Tara wasn't even aware she had spoken out loud, that she had told Clay and Johnny where all her pain was coming from. She was inconsolable and was unaware of the two men watching her and becoming very worried. She was oblivious of Clay turning to Johnny and mouthing the words, "Call Doc." She was also unaware that Clay was worried Tara was going to make herself ill. Clay was relieved when Johnny advised Doc was on his way and listened as Johnny told him Doc Foster had been out on a house call at the neighboring ranch. Clay sighed when Doc arrived moments later. Clay saw Doc take in the scene with a worried frown, grasp his medical bag, and set up a needle. He injected the sedative into Tara's arm and watched as her crying slowed until she was asleep on his lap.

"Put Tara to bed and then come into the kitchen," Doc commanded, and Clay watched as Doc walked from the room..

Clay walked into the kitchen and stood behind an empty chair near where Johnny and Doc were already seated and watched as the elderly doctor rose again and helped himself to a cup of coffee.

"Sit down," Doc stated quietly. "What in tarnation is going on? Why was that poor girl in such a state?"

Clay spent the next half an hour telling Doc Foster all about what Tara had sobbed out in her hysterical state, Johnny interrupting Clay every now and then with pieces of the story he'd forgotten to tell. Doc never said a word, just sat back and listened. When Clay had finished his telling, Clay tried not to cringe as Doc leaned forward and he knew he was about to read them the riot act.

"How the hell could you do that to that little girl when she is in such a fragile state? You two should be ashamed of yourselves. You need to give that girl time to get over her grief and shock. From the sounds of things, she hasn't had a minute to spare to grieve for her mother. She is going to end up having a nervous breakdown if you don't back off. Instead of trying to force that child, woo her. Take her horse riding, take her out to dinner. Give her some of the fun that has been missing from her life for so long. I know you didn't mean to shock her out of her amnesia or to hurt her in any way, but you have to build her self-esteem up again before you can expect her to accept a relationship with one or both of you. She's been alone and had no one but herself to rely on," Doc stated as he rose to his feet and walked to the door then turned around to face the Clay and his brother once more. "Call me if you need to."

"Fuck it. What have we done, Johnny? We never should have treated Tara that way. I was thinking with my dick and not with my head."

"You and me both, Clay. We are both responsible for the way Tara just fell apart. We're going to have to treat her like fragile glass until she feels more herself. Fuck. What if she never wants anything to do with us again after the way we treated her?"

"I don't know, Johnny. I just don't know."

Chapter Nine

Tara stood staring out of the bedroom window as the first rays of the sun chased away the darkness of the night. She had been sitting in the window seat and was still dressed, with a blanket thrown over her shoulders. The memories of the previous afternoon came crashing back through her mind, making her cheeks flame with embarrassment. She couldn't believe she had lost control like that. She remembered Johnny trying to talk to her, and she had yelled at him, furious for making her feel again.

Tara threw the blanket from her body and walked farther into the room. Apart from feeling a little woozy and her eyes feeling twice their usual size, swollen from her crying jag, she actually felt better than she had for a long, long time. She had always heard that crying was cathartic, but had never really believed it. She gave a sigh and went to the bathroom for a shower.

Tara entered the kitchen to find Clay and Johnny sitting at the kitchen table drinking coffee and eating breakfast. She smiled at them as they looked at her, and then she walked over to the coffee, poured herself a mug, and sat down at the table.

"How are you feeling, Tara?" Clay asked as he and his brother scrutinized her face.

"I'm fine."

"Do you want to go for a ride today, sweetheart?" Johnny asked from the other side of the table.

"Yes, please. I have missed riding so much," Tara replied wistfully.

"What do you want for breakfast, baby?" asked Clay.

"I'm good."

"We are not leaving until you've got something in your stomach, Tara. So what will it be?" Clay asked again as he stood and went to the kitchen.

"Sit down, Clay. I can get my own breakfast. In fact, I'm supposed to be doing all the cooking around here," Tara replied as she went to the toaster to make herself some toast.

"Is toast all you're gonna have, Tara? That's not enough food to start the day," Johnny opined as he pushed his plate aside.

"It's enough for me since I've only been eating once a day." Tara could have bitten her tongue off for revealing that little tidbit of information.

"That is going to change right now, Tara. You are to eat three meals a day. You're way too skinny as it is. If I find out you're skipping meals, I'll put you over my knee and tan your ass," Clay stated.

"And I'll help him," Johnny advised.

"Ooh, I'm so scared of the big, bad, mean cowboys," Tara replied with a smirk.

Tara saw Johnny and Clay look at each other and knew they didn't know what to make of Tara's statement. She was back to feeling more like her sassy self but knew by their expressions and body language they weren't willing to push her too hard, too fast in case she had a relapse and broke down again.

Tara brought her toast to the table and began to eat, aware of the two masculine, sexy cowboys eying her. She couldn't help the grin that spread across her face, and then she was laughing out loud at the two astonished men. It looked like they didn't know how to treat her anymore. Maybe they were too scared she would burst into tears again. Hmm, she might be able to use that to her advantage.

"Are you goading us, little girl?" Clay asked with narrowed eyes.

"Would I do that?" Tara replied with a smile that wouldn't melt butter.

"I do believe you would. Just remember, we are bigger, stronger, and a lot meaner than you'll ever be, sweet," Johnny replied with a smile. And Tara knew he was happy to see the life back in her eyes.

Tara finished her toast, collected all the dishes, put them in the dishwasher, wiped down the counters and the table, and turned back to Clay and Johnny.

"So, which horse do I get to ride?"

"Come on out to the barn and take your pick. Actually, how long has it been since you've ridden, baby?" asked Clay.

"The last time was with you two."

"Okay, we'll give you Pepper to ride, since she's more docile. No, Tara, don't argue. Until I know you're back up to par with your riding, you get Pepper," Clay stated.

"Okay. Let's go, time's a-wasting," Tara said as she grabbed hold of Clay's hand to drag him from the house.

They rode out of the yard to the west of the property. Tara hadn't felt so free and alive in a long time. She loved the scents of the cypress trees, animals, and wildflowers growing sporadically in the paddocks. She kicked Pepper into a canter, and with the exhilaration flowing through her veins, she upped the pace until she and Pepper were galloping across the fields. She laughed out loud. She had missed the freedom of riding a horse in the country. She was finally free from the hustle and bustle of a city. She never wanted to go back to that horrible, lonely place. She slowed Pepper to a canter and then a walk as she cooled the animal beneath her down, Clay and Johnny on either side of her.

"You have no idea how much I've missed this. Thank you. Both of you," Tara said gratefully.

"It's our pleasure, Tara. We just want you to be happy," Clay replied.

"You know what? For the first time in eight years, I am happy, and it's thanks to you two. Let's go paddle in the stream, then we'd better head back so I can make you two pigs some lunch. Oink, oink, oink."

"Oh, you are so going to pay for that, sweetheart," Johnny said with a grin.

"Yeah, yeah, I know. You're gonna put me over your knees and tan my ass. You have to catch me first," Tara said over her shoulder as she nudged Pepper into a gallop once more.

Tara rode into the yard to see a car parked near the house. The woman that got out of the small, expensive car made Tara feel really dowdy. She wore a feminine, sophisticated dress, which hugged her voluptuous curves, and the heels she teetered on across the yard were so high it was a wonder she didn't twist her ankle and break it. Tara ignored the woman and rode Pepper into the barn. She dismounted, removed the saddle, and backed Pepper into her stall. She removed the bridle and then began the process of rubbing Pepper down and currying her with the specialized comb. She made sure Pepper had water and then left the barn to head for the house. Tara was halfway across the yard when she heard the woman speak.

"I've missed you so much, Clay. Why haven't you been to see me?"

"I told you before, we're done, Celia. Why do you keep coming out here?"

"Come on, Clay. You, me, and Johnny had such a good thing going. Why do you want to throw it away?"

Tara didn't wait around to hear the reply. Just when she was feeling on top of the world again, that bitch had to turn up. She knew Johnny and Clay were healthy, sexual men and wouldn't have waited around for her, but having the situation right in her face made pain stab into her heart.

Tara washed her hands at the sink and set about making omelettes and salad for lunch with warm crusty rolls from the oven. By the time Clay and Johnny entered the kitchen, everything was set out on the table ready to eat.

Tara sat and ate quietly. She wasn't interested in making small talk to the two men seated at the table with her. She kept her eyes on her plate, not willing to have the confrontation she knew would come if they could discern her thoughts. When Clay spoke, it seemed that wasn't necessary anyway. He seemed to be able to read her mind.

"Celia meant nothing to us, Tara. We used her and she used us. She knew from the start nothing would eventuate from a relationship with us. She was a means to scratch an itch, to fuck. You mean so much more to us than that," Clay stated as he leaned over the table, placed a finger beneath her chin to make her look at him.

"And that's supposed to make me feel better? You have a lot to learn about women if you think that explanation is supposed to make me feel better," Tara stated with ire, rose from her chair, and left the dining room.

Tara couldn't believe how callously he had treated that woman. Didn't that mean they treated all women the same? Including her? She waited until she heard the slam of the back door then went to clean up the kitchen. She gave a sigh of relief to find it empty and set about putting the kitchen to rights and preparing food for dinner. Once that was done, she went on a cleaning frenzy. By the time she had to put dinner in the oven, the house was spotless. Tara had cleaned the whole house from top to bottom, including the bathrooms and the floors. She put the chicken casserole in the oven and set the rice boiler to start in about forty minutes, and then she went to shower.

Tara was back in the kitchen ready to serve dinner when Clay and Johnny entered the back door.

"You've got five minutes to clean up. Dinner's ready, and if I hold it off any longer it will start to spoil," Tara stated without turning around. She heard their footsteps as they left to shower and change.

Tara served dinner and was just placing the plates on the table as Clay and Johnny returned. She wanted nothing more than to pick up her plate and hide in her bedroom, but knew she would be hauled back to the dining room, so she didn't bother. She sat down and picked at her food, listening as Clay and Johnny talked about the ranch. When Tara couldn't stomach the thought of another mouthful of food, she picked her plate up, stood, and took it over to the kitchen.

She was just about to scrape the food into the trash as a large hand plucked the plate from hers, put it down on the counter, and turned her around gently by the shoulders.

Tara felt Johnny's finger beneath her chin, lifting her gaze to his. She knew he could see the pain and sadness, which was not there this morning, back in her eyes and face. He picked her up in his arms and carried her back to the table, sat down with her on his lap within the circle of his arms.

"Talk to me, Tara. What happened between our horse ride and now to make you so sad?"

Tara kept her eyes on the table, not wanting him or Clay to know she was envious of their previous and or current lovers. She'd felt as if her heart was breaking all over again when she had seen Celia hanging off her men and talking to them.

"Celia," Clay stated from next to her. "That's what this is about, isn't it, baby?"

"Is Clay right, sweetheart? You have nothing to worry about, Tara. You are the one we want. The women we had previously in our lives, before you showed up again, meant nothing. They were just a fuck, Tara, they didn't mean anything," Johnny explained.

Tara pushed Johnny's arms from around her waist, rose to her feet, and moved a few paces away. She turned back to face Clay and Johnny head-on. She'd had enough of this shit.

"So was I just a fuck, too? Another warm body to relieve an itch?" Tara asked with a sneer on her face, trying to cover the pain inside her.

"Is that what you think? God, Tara, don't you know how much you mean to us? We love you, baby. We have loved you since you were fifteen years old. But there was nothing we could do about it. Don't you understand that? We were so much older than you. We still are, but at least you're of age now. Nothing will ever stop us from loving you," Clay verbalized as he rose from his chair, moving toward her with a predatory glean in his eyes, Johnny following close behind him.

"Do you really mean that? You're not just saying it to make me feel better?"

"No, sweetheart. We never say anything we don't mean. You should know that, Tara. How could you think we didn't love you?" Johnny asked, anguish evident in his voice.

"I thought you liked me like a sister. How was I to know it was more than that? You never told me."

"Oh, baby. We wanted to. So damn much, but we couldn't. You were way too young. We were waiting for you to grow up, and then nothing was going to hold us back," Clay stated as he drew Tara into his arms. Tara sighed as he pulled her up against the length of his body, holding her tightly against him. She glanced over her shoulder when she felt Johnny move in behind her, leaning his body against Tara's back, sandwiching her between them, and felt his brother wrap his arms around Tara's hips.

"I love you, too. I love both of you so much. I thought I'd die not being with you when Mom and I had to move. And when I came to say good-bye, found you both fucking that woman, it broke my heart. I felt like I would shatter. I wanted to get in touch with you, but I didn't think you cared anymore." Tara sobbed. She clutched Clay's shirt in her hand and let the warmth of their large, muscular bodies seep into her cold frame. She felt her heart open wide and fill with joy and happiness. She had finally come home. She was complete for once in her life. Complete like she never had been before.

"How about you go and strip off your clothes and lay on the bed, sweetheart? Clay and I want to give you a massage so your muscles don't freeze up after riding this morning."

"Okay. That would be nice."

"Go on then, baby. We'll be in in a minute," Clay said as he released Tara, turned her toward the hallway, and popped her on the ass.

Tara exited the kitchen with a smile and an extra sway in her hips. Her smile broadened as she heard Clay and Johnny groan behind her.

Chapter Ten

Tara grabbed a large, clean towel out of the bathroom cupboard, stripped her clothes off, and settled on top of the towel on the bed. She gave a sigh and let the tension in her muscles drain away as she rested her head on the back of her hands She heard footsteps in the hall and knew Clay and Johnny were about to enter the room.

"Wow, do you know how sexy you are, Tara? You take my breath away." Clay growled as he walked to the side of the bed.

"I've never felt sexy before, but you two make me feel beautiful and sexy. I love you both so much," Tara replied with a hitch in her voice.

"We love you, too, sweetheart. And you are the sexiest little thing I've ever seen. You make me so hard, Tara," Johnny stated in a deep, husky, passion-filled voice. "Now we are going to give you a nice massage and then we're going to show you how much we love you. We want you to just lay back and relax, let us give you some pampering, honey. Okay?"

"Okay."

Tara heard the pop of a bottle, and then the sweet scent of avocado and honey filled the air. Large, warm, oily hands connected with her shoulders and ran down along her back and spine, massaging the tight knots of muscle until they released. Another pair of hands began to massage her thighs and legs and slowly crept up to her buttocks. Tara couldn't help groaning at the pleasure-pain of her muscles being massaged. She could have lain there for hours, floating in and out of a doze as they eased her tension.

The air in the room began to thicken as her butt cheeks were massaged and separated with eroticism then the large warm hands ran up and down the inside of her thighs. Tara's breathing began to escalate as the two pairs of hands wandered up and down the length of her body. They spent a lot of time on her, getting her to relax, but also turning her on until she could feel her pussy weeping her juices onto the inside of her thighs.

"Turn over, baby," Clay commanded quietly as he held her hips to help her turn.

She opened her eyes, her lids heavy with passion as she took in Johnny, then Clay. She watched as they poured more oil into their hands then rubbed them together to warm the oil. Clay reached for her shoulders and began to massage, moving his large palms down over her until her breasts were beneath his slippery hands. He kneaded the mounds of flesh gently but firmly, making sure to flick his thumbs over her hard nipples.

Johnny started from the tops of her feet and worked his way up the length of her legs. He moved up the outside of her limbs, gliding his hands back down over the top of them, then worked his way up the inside of her thighs.

Tara arched her breasts and hips up to those delicious, massaging palms, trying to get them to touch her where she needed them most. Johnny and Clay chuckled and moved their hands away from her breasts and legs to meet on her abdomen. They removed their hands, wiped them off on a hand towel, and began to remove their clothes as they watched her.

"If you don't want this, baby, now is the time to say something," Clay growled out.

Tara looked from Clay to Johnny, giving them a saucy smile and wink. She laughed out loud as the two men removed their clothes, lightning fast. Johnny finished first and crawled up onto the bed on her left side. He held her gaze with his own and slowly lowered his head down to hers. He slid his lips over her mouth, groaning with pleasure when Tara slid her tongue over his top lip. Johnny angled his head and devoured her mouth.

Tara mewled as Johnny slid his tongue into her mouth, gliding it along hers as they twirled and fought for supremacy of the kiss. Johnny won by pushing her tongue back into her mouth using his own. The sensation as he nipped and licked at her lips as their mouths mated was so wonderful she wanted more, and she whimpered with frustration as he finally drew back from the kiss when the need for air necessitated. She heard him gulp air into his own lungs and watched as he turned his head to see Clay sucking her nipple into his mouth while he pinched the other hard peak between his thumb and finger.

Her breath hitched as Johnny crawled down to the end of the bed, spread Tara's thighs wide, and moved up between them. She couldn't believe what he did next. He lay down on his belly and breathed the scent of her weeping pussy into his nose. It looked as if he enjoyed her scent as a wicked grin slid over his lips, and then he was lowering his head. He moved his head down and licked her from her small, creamy hole, up through her folds to her clit. The little bundle of nerves was standing up, begging him for attention.

Tara felt Clay release her nipple from his mouth with a pop and then lean up to take her mouth with his. He slammed his mouth over hers and ate at her lips until she opened her mouth to give him the access he wanted. He gentled the kiss and took her mouth with a languid slowness that had Tara begging for more. She groaned into his mouth as he poured all of his love into his kiss. She had never wanted a man or men the way she wanted Clay and Johnny. They made her feel complete and comfortable in her own skin. He weaned his mouth from hers and lifted his head to watch Johnny consume her pussy.

Tara couldn't prevent a groan from escaping as Johnny pushed two fingers into her hot, wet cunt as his tongue swirled and laved over her clit. He twisted his fingers around and slid them up to the top of her pussy walls to the second knuckle until he found what he was searching for. The sensation of him rubbing the pads of his fingers over the rough patch of flesh inside her pussy had her moaning even more, and she heard Johnny give a chuckle as she bucked her hips up, eager for more of his touch. She felt Johnny place a large palm across her lower abdomen and pubic bone to hold her hips down. He moved his fingers in and out of her pussy faster as he laved his tongue over her clit. She couldn't stop herself from moaning with pleasure and felt the walls of her wet sheath ripple around his fingers. Johnny began to pump his fingers in and out, faster, harder, and deeper, making sure to slide over her G-spot and give a slight tug at the top of her pussy near the entrance. She felt him push down on her pubic bone harder to keep her from bucking him off of her, and her moaning was became louder and longer, indicating she was moments away from climax. She saw Johnny open his eyes just in time for both of them to see Clay suck one of her hard nipples into his mouth as he pinched the other one between his finger and thumb.

Tara heard Johnny give a moan of satisfaction when her cunt clamped down hard on his fingers and filled his mouth and the palm of his hand with her cum. He growled deep in his throat as he sucked and licked her juices up into his mouth, making lewd slurping sounds. It was like he couldn't get enough of her sweet cream. He always seemed so eager to eat her pussy out, and she knew he could spend hours doing so if she would only let him. He told her as much early this morning. He kept thrusting his cock and balls against her thigh, and she knew he was aching as much as she was. He was as eager as she to have his flesh buried deep in her cunt.

Tara was panting heavily as she felt Johnny move up between her legs, lean over her, and take her mouth with his, getting even more turned on as he shared the taste of her cum with her. He pushed his hips into hers, making both of them groan when she felt the head of his cock slip through the tight flesh of her pussy. He slid his tongue into her mouth, twining it with hers as he thrust his hips forward again, another couple of inches of his cock slipping into her tight sheath. Tara knew he was trying to go slow, but she was having none of that. She grabbed his ass and bucked her hips up into his, and he plunged into her until he was buried balls-deep.

Tara gripped Johnny's ass tighter as he weaned his mouth from hers, slid his arms up underneath her shoulders, and pulled her up, making her release her hold on him, until they were breast to chest, with her sitting impaled on his hard rod. He spread his legs and grasped her fleshy, muscular cheeks and spread them wide. Tara felt Clay move up behind her and massage some of the fragrant oil into the small pucker of her anus. He pushed and tantalized the sensitive nerves until she relaxed her muscles as her ass opened up to him, letting him know she liked what he was doing. He slowly eased his fingers into her tight ass, and Tara turned her head just in time to see him bite his lip as if to keep himself in control of his own body. Once his fingers were all the way in her tight, dark entrance, he wiggled his fingers around, stretching her tight muscles. She could feel him slowly scissoring his fingers as he began to pump his digits in and out of her dark entrance. Then she started trying to push back on his fingers, letting him know she was ready for him. He withdrew his fingers from her butt, causing her to groan, but then she heard the slick sound of him lathering his cock with more oil, and he moved in close to her body once more.

Tara groaned as Clay held her waist while Johnny held her butt cheeks wide for him. He slowly began to push his hard cock into her body. He moaned loudly as the tip of his penis pushed through the tight muscles of her sphincter.

"Oh God, what are you doing to me? It burns. You're hurting me," Tara gasped out.

"Do you want me to stop, baby?" Clay asked, holding his breath, waiting for her reply.

"No, I want you to fuck me," Tara cried out.

"Breathe, sweetheart. That's it. Breathe in and out with me, and when Clay starts to push in again, use your muscles to push out," Johnny whispered in her ear.

Clay began to push in again, so Tara breathed and pushed her ass muscles out. She groaned as Clay slid into her ass. The pain was too much to bear, until all of a sudden the feeling changed to pleasure.

"I'm in, baby. Good girl. God, you are so sexy. Now don't move, Tara, let Johnny and I do all the work. We don't want to hurt you," Clay advised.

Clay pulled his cock back until just the tip was resting inside her ass. As he pushed back in, Johnny pulled his engorged meat out of her tight, wet pussy until he was just resting inside her body. They set a slow, easy rhythm, making sure not to hurt Tara in any way. With each thrust of their hips, they slowly increased the pace until Tara couldn't stand it anymore. She began rocking her hips in time with their thrusts until she had them moving in and out of her body in a faster pace. The sound of their balls slapping against her flesh heightened her arousal to a fever pitch. She felt the first tingles warning of her impending climax as her wall rippled along the hard flesh sliding in and out of her body.

"It's too much. You have to stop," Tara cried.

"No, sweetheart. Don't hold back. We want you to come on our cocks. Let go, Tara. Milk the seed from our balls," Johnny panted against her ear.

Tara grunted as Clay moved a hand down between her and Johnny's body. Without touching his brother, he wet the pad of his finger in her pussy juice and slid back up to her clit. He rubbed his finger over the hard bundle of nerves a few times until she was screaming and bucking between them. She couldn't prevent her body from clamping down hard on their dicks. She had them groaning out loud as they forged in and out of her body. They pumped into her body a couple more times, and she was satisfied to hear them both roar their release as she pulled them into space with her, her cunt still convulsing around their hard cocks. When her body stopped clenching and slowly came back down to earth, Tara flopped her head onto Johnny's shoulder, breathing rapidly until her lungs stopped working so hard.

Tara gave a soft sigh as Clay slowly eased his softening cock from her ass, which then had them both groaning. He bent down and scooped her up, pulling her off Johnny's cock, and headed to the bathroom.

"Hey. I was enjoying our cuddle," Johnny stated belligerently as he followed Clay into the bathroom.

"Too bad," Clay replied as he sat on the edge of the large spa bath, put the plug in, and started the water. When the water was halfway up the side of the tub, he stood up with Tara still in his arms and sat down on one of the molded seats, placing Tara onto his lap.

"How are you feeling, baby?"

"Sore."

"Just sit there and relax, sweetheart," Johnny advised as he stepped into the tub. "Clay and I will wash you, then we'll let the spa jets do the rest."

"Okay," Tara replied as she closed her eyes.

She had never felt so good in her life. Even though her muscles and ass were a little sore, she felt content and loved for the first time in years.

Chapter Eleven

Tara had never been so happy. She kept the house clean, cooked for her two men, and did the laundry. They spent a couple of hours with her each morning, taking her for a ride, reacquainting her with her childhood home. They were in a routine, and she had never seen Clay and Johnny as happy as they were.

One Friday afternoon, after she had done all her chores and dinner and was cooking in the slow cooker, Tara decided to go for another ride on Pepper. She walked out the back door and was headed for the barn when she heard the sound of a car coming up the drive. She covered her eyes with her hands to see who was visiting and felt anger rising as she recognized Celia's expensive sports car. Tara moved away from the driveway so she wouldn't be in the way of the woman speeding down the drive.

Tara realized too late that Celia was not going to slow down. She was headed straight for her. Tara spun on her heels and ran for her life. The car swerved at the last moment, and then she was flying though the air. The impact of the front quarter panel on her left leg had her screaming out in pain. Tara landed on the ground in agony. She couldn't move or speak as tears coursed down her face. She felt sick to her stomach with pain. Tara was aware of Celia turning her car around and speeding off back up the driveway.

One of the ranch hands must have heard Tara scream, because he came running out of the barn and crouched down beside her.

"Tara, are you all right? What happened?" Steve asked.

Tara could see he was looking at the car as it fishtailed up the driveway in the distance.

"Leg, Celia, car, broke."

"Take it easy, Tara. I'm going to call an ambulance then I'll call Johnny and Clay. I'll be back with a blanket for you," Steve said then took off at a run.

He was back in moments, covering Tara with several blankets as she was going into shock. Her teeth were chattering, and her body was shaking so much she couldn't keep her head up. She saw Steve on his cell phone and watched as he pulled his jacket off to place it underneath her head.

Tara had no idea how long she lay on the ground. It could have been minutes, or hours. The next thing she knew, she heard the siren from an ambulance and a rumble of horses' hooves vibrating over the ground. She heard the roar of fury from Clay and Johnny and turned her head just in time to see them both leaping from their mounts.

"Tara, what's happened, baby?" Clay asked as he got down on his knees beside her.

"Sweetheart, what's wrong?" Johnny asked as he got down on her other side.

"Celia, she hit me with her car. I think my leg is broken," Tara cried.

The ambulance pulled up on the drive right next to her. Two paramedics jumped out of the vehicle and rushed over to Tara.

"Excuse me, sirs, we need to assess the young lady for injuries. Could you please move back?"

Clay and Johnny moved back and sat down on the ground above Tara's head. The two paramedics assessed her for damage. One of the paramedics ran to the van and retrieved an inflatable leg splint. He gently placed it on Tara's leg and inflated it to prevent her from moving and injuring her leg. The man who had brought the splint ran to the van once more and pulled out a stretcher. He lowered it down to the lowest possible setting, and then he and his partner placed a back board beneath Tara's body.

"On three. One, two, three, lift." The two men lifted Tara and slid her onto the portable stretcher.

"Are you taking Tara to Slick Rock?" Clay asked.

"Yes, sir. The clinic has been set up, ready and waiting for the young lady. Would one of you like to ride in with us?"

"Yes. Is it all right if I go, Johnny?" Clay asked his brother.

"I don't care which one of us goes, as long as Tara isn't alone. Go, Clay. I won't be far behind you."

Tara saw Clay following the paramedics to the vehicle, watching their every move as they carefully slid her into the back. He followed the paramedic into the back of the van, moved out of the way up to Tara's head. He knelt on the floor beside her and placed a kiss on her forehead.

"I'm just going to give you a shot for the pain, Tara. All right?" the paramedic asked.

Tara was in too much pain to answer, so she nodded her head in affirmation. Nearly as soon as the paramedic had given her the pain relief, her eyes became too heavy to hold open. She gave a sigh and let them slide closed. She was vaguely aware of Clay holding on to one of her hands as the vehicle moved over the bitumen. By the time they arrived at the clinic, she was deeply asleep.

* * * *

Clay met her eyes as she looked at him through a drug-induced haze and was glad she had been given the pain medication. He could see the resignation on her face and knew she was aware as well as he that her leg was broken and needed to be reset. He was glad she'd had the shot which would dull the excruciating pain she would have felt if she hadn't had the pain medication. Clay followed the paramedics as they wheeled her into the clinic to find Doc Foster waiting for them. He walked beside Tara as they took her into the big consulting room then watched carefully as they slid her over onto a bed and left. Clay helped Tara to concentrate on him as the Doc worked by holding her hand. He watched Doc cut her jeans away from her left leg after he removed the inflatable splint, and then wheeled the bed over to the X-ray machine with his help.

Doc and Clay stood behind the protective radiation barrier as the machine began to scan her leg. When it was done, Doc looked on the computer on the other side of the room while Clay placed a blanket over Tara.

"Well, it's not a full break, but she does have a fracture, and as you saw, a lot of bruising. What the hell happened, Clay? It looks like she was hit by a car," Doc asked as he moved away from the computer and began preparing plaster.

"I think she was, Doc. She's in so much pain she couldn't speak properly, but she managed to say, Celia, car, something like that. I want to question her, but I wanted to wait until after she'd had medical treatment."

"Hmm, well, by the time I've finished putting a cast on her leg from her foot to just below her knee, she should be coming out of her drugged stupor. I hope she doesn't come around until then. I don't want to cause Tara any more unnecessary pain."

Doc got down to the business of placing a plaster cast on Tara's leg under the careful eye of Clay. By the time he was finished, Tara was coming out of her medication haze.

"Hey, baby, how are you feeling?" Clay asked a groggy Tara.

"Like, I got hit by a car."

"Can you tell me what happened, Tara?" Doc Foster asked as he stood to his feet.

"I was heading to the barn and was halfway across the yard on the driveway when I heard a car coming. I looked up to see who it was and finally realized it was Celia. She was driving like a maniac, speeding down the driveway. I stood watching her and finally realized she wasn't slowing down and she was heading right for me. I tried to get out of her way, but obviously I wasn't fast enough. What's the damage, Doc?"

"You have a hairline fracture on your left tibia. I've had to put your lower leg in a cast so you don't do any more damage. We should be able to remove the cast in about six weeks. Do you want me to report the incident, Clay, or would you rather do it?" Doc asked.

"I'll do it," he replied.

"All right then. I am going to write you out a prescription for some pain medication, young lady. You are going to need it. I have a pair of crutches in another room we lend out from time to time which should be about the right height for you. If the swelling in your leg gets too bad and it feels like the plaster is cutting into you, come and see me straight away. Do you need me to call anyone to come get you?" asked Doc.

"No, thanks anyway, Doc. Johnny's probably already out in the waiting room pacing a hole in your carpet," Clay replied.

"Okay, I'll go and get Johnny to pull his vehicle around to the back of the office so you can get this young lady into the back. You can take that blanket with you to keep warm. No moving around too much for the next couple of days, all right?"

"Thanks, Doc," Tara replied.

"Yeah, thanks," Clay said.

"Give Johnny five minutes to move his truck, and then you can go," Doc stated.

Clay waited the five minutes with Tara in the consulting room, making sure she was covered with the blanket and comfortable enough, even though she was still in pain. Clay looked up when the door opened to see Johnny standing in the doorway and scooped Tara up into his arms and headed for the door. Clay stopped when his brother spoke to Tara.

"How are you feeling, sweetheart? Are you in too much pain?" Johnny asked with concern.

"No, I'm okay. Thanks, Johnny," Tara replied.

"We need to get Tara home so she'll be more comfortable, Johnny. I want you to call the sheriff and get him to meet us at the ranch."

Clay saw Johnny give Tara a kiss on the head and walked out the back door of Doc's office. He opened the back door to the truck and got into the backseat so he could guide Tara's plaster-encased limb.

* * * *

Johnny knew Tara was grateful he made sure her leg didn't hit anything as Clay slid her in onto the backseat because she thanked them both. He heard her sigh when he carefully placed a travel pillow beneath her foot and another beneath her knee, keeping her leg propped up so she couldn't hurt herself. Johnny got out the other side of the car and saw his brother gently close the back door for her to lean against.

"I'll drive, Johnny, you get in the front passenger seat and keep an eye on Tara. Call the sheriff so we can report Celia for a hit and run. I want her charged as soon as possible, but Luke is going to want to come out and take a statement from Tara," Clay stated in a hard voice.

Johnny saw Clay get into the driver's seat and start the vehicle as he walked around to the front and got into the passenger side. He pulled on his seat belt and took out his cell phone to call the sheriff while he sat half-sideways in his seat to keep an eye on Tara. He saw Clay turn his head to see their woman once more, and then turned back to the front before his brother put the stick into gear and drove from the parking lot.

Her face was so pale Johnny had to physically stop himself from crawling into the backseat with her and taking her into his arms. He didn't want to hurt her by jostling her around too much.

Johnny kept his eyes on Tara the whole time he talked to the sheriff on the drive home and knew that Luke Sun-Walker would be at the ranch very soon to take Tara's statement. He gave a sigh as Clay pulled the truck along close to the front steps to the deck.

Johnny got out of the car, and he carefully opened the back door Tara was leaning against. He placed his large hand into the small gap in the door to stop her from tumbling out, as she was still under the influence of her pain meds. He waited for Clay to get in the backseat to guide Tara's plastered leg so they wouldn't hurt her then lifted her carefully into his arms. He walked up the steps to the house and carried Tara into the living room with Clay going ahead of him to hold the door open.

Johnny and Clay had just settled Tara on the sofa with a pillow beneath her head, another beneath her knee and foot, with a blanket over the top of her, when a knock sounded on the door. Clay left to answer the door.

"Do you want a drink or anything, sweetheart?" Clay asked.

"Yes, please. Can I have a glass of water and a cup of coffee?" Tara mumbled sleepily.

"Sure thing, sweetheart. I'll be back in a minute."

"Tara," Clay called as he walked back into the living room. "I'd like you to meet the sheriff, Luke Sun-Walker. Luke, this is Tara Rustle."

"Hi, Tara, pleased to meet you," Luke stated.

"You, too, Sheriff."

"Take a load off, Luke. I'll bring in some coffee while you talk to Tara," Clay said.

"Here you go, sweetheart," Clay said as he pulled a small side table around in front of Tara and placed the glass of water on it. He handed Luke a cup of coffee and disappeared into the kitchen. He was back in moments with everyone's coffee.

"Tara, can you tell me what happened? How did you break your leg?" Luke asked gently.

Tara gave her statement to Luke, relating all the details of the incident.

"Okay. Thanks for your statement, Tara. I'll get an APB out on Celia."

Johnny watched Tara pick up the water and guzzle it down. He was astounded at how quickly she finished the water. She must have been thirsty and finally twigged the pain medication Doc had given her probably made her mouth feel dry. He watched as she carefully placed the glass back on the table, ready to help her if necessary, and then she reached for her coffee mug and tried to sit up a little more to drink her hot beverage. Johnny moved and reached her before Clay. He took the coffee from her hand and placed it on the table then turned back to her. Johnny and Clay helped her into a more comfortable position. Johnny held her injured leg still while Clay placed his arms beneath her armpits. When she was more comfortable, Johnny smiled and gave her a pat on the shoulder, and Tara thanked them and grabbed for her coffee cup as he handed it back to her.

Johnny kept an eye on Tara as she listened to them talking about the ranch and the need for more employees at the Sheriff's department. Slick Rock was beginning to become more populated as more and more people got out of the hustle and bustle of the cities. He took the mug from Tara when she finished her coffee, placed the mug on the table, and saw her eyes slide closed. Johnny indicated to Clay and Luke to lower their voices and gave a sigh of relief as Tara's breathing evened and deepened. She had finally drifted off to sleep.

Chapter Twelve

The next two days passed in a blur of pain for Tara. Clay and Johnny never left her side, and she felt guilty about keeping them from their ranch work. On the third day, Tara's pain was at a much more manageable level, and she was determined to be up and about. All she had to do was learn to use the crutches Doc had sent home with her. Piece of cake. Or so she thought.

Johnny and Clay stood by Tara as she tried to use the crutches, one on either side of her in case she fell. She started out wobbly, but by the end of the day, she found a rhythm and felt much more confident using the apparatus. She was beginning to get cabin fever and wanted to be able to get outside to sit on the decking. She had been sitting on the sofa for the last two days and was utterly sick of it.

She was fine until she got to the door. She leaned over and pushed the door open, but by the time she was ready to step forward, the door had already closed again. Tara wanted to scream with frustration, but didn't give in to that childish display. And she also didn't want Clay and Johnny running to help her again. She needed to learn to move about without any help. An idea formed in her mind, which made her smile. She pushed the screen door open so it wasn't latched and then just plowed through it, using her elbow to push the screen door away from her body. Once outside, she moved her elbow, watched with satisfaction as the door slammed closed behind her, and then slowly went to sit on the padded bench seat. She gave a sigh as she breathed in the crisp, clean country air with a hint of roses floating in the breeze from the other side of the house. Tara gingerly lifted her plaster-encased leg up to rest it along the seat and sat back in the corner to enjoy the peace and quiet.

"Tara, where are you?" Clay yelled from inside the house.

Tara sighed, knowing she was going to have to answer and would end up getting a lecture from Clay, but she didn't want him worrying over her.

"I'm outside, Clay," she yelled in reply.

Clay came storming out of the house, and she heard the fast, frantic footsteps of Johnny following close behind.

"What the hell do you think you're doing? If you weren't already hurt, I would put you over my knee and tan your ass. You know you're not supposed to be moving around by yourself. What if you had fallen and hurt your leg even more?" Clay asked through clenched teeth.

"Then I would have hurt my leg. Look, Clay, Johnny, you can't be treating me like a fragile piece of glass. I'm a lot stronger than you think. I just needed to get out of the house for some fresh air. I was going stir crazy staying inside all the time. I have to learn to get around by myself. What if there was an emergency on the ranch and you and Johnny had to leave? I wouldn't even be able to go to the bathroom by myself. Stop pampering me. It's not that I don't appreciate it, because I do, I love you both very much, but you're both driving me insane."

"She's right, Clay. She does have to learn to get around. We can't be here twenty-four-seven, even though we'd like to. We have to let her move about on her own. How about I get you a cell phone and program our numbers into it? That way if we're not here you can still get in touch with us if you need to."

"I think that's a great idea, Johnny. What do you say, Clay? You can't be with me all the time," Tara reiterated.

"Yeah, okay. So you have a point. Johnny, go for a quick run into Slick Rock and get Tara a cell phone. I'll stay here and keep her company. Is there anything else you want in town, baby?"

"Something to read would be nice, and a new leg?" Tara replied with spunk.

"What am I going to do with you, Tara?"

"Love me, Clay. Just love me."

"I already do, baby." Clay leaned down and kissed her on the cheek.

Johnny followed suit and placed a gentle kiss on her lips then turned toward his truck with a wave over his shoulder.

Clay sat down on a chair beside Tara and they sat companionably, listening to the twittering of the birds and the ranch animals. Tara hated being cooped up inside. She had always loved being outside, especially when her dad was around. All he and her mom ever seemed to do was fight. Staying outside and far away from the house when she was growing up was her sanity. She had spent way more time with Clay and Johnny than her own parents. It wasn't that she didn't love them, it was just she couldn't stand to hear them fighting all the time.

Tara closed her eyes and drifted in her mind. Thinking about the family she wanted with Clay and Johnny. Hoping one day one or both of them would ask her to marry them. She didn't want to have to choose between the men she loved and hoped they never asked her to. She'd always dreamed of having Johnny and Clay by her side. Even as a young girl she used to envisage her two men coming home to her after working all day on the ranch. She would have dinner ready for them and serve it as they washed up. They would talk over their days as they ate, and after she had cleared up, her men would carry her off to the bedroom to make love to her all night long. Eventually there would be children to nurture and care for. Her need to love and be loved for who she was, unconditionally, would be fulfilled. That's all she'd every really wanted in life, to love and be loved in return. She felt her heart expand as the thoughts drifting by filled her heart to overflowing with love.

Johnny was back from town a lot faster than she expected him to be, and she watched as he walked up the decking steps with a frown on his face.

"What's wrong, Johnny? Were you able to get a phone?" asked Tara.

"Yeah. I'll just go inside and set it up for you, sweetheart," Johnny replied as he entered the house.

Tara saw Johnny thrust his chin forward to Clay, indicating he wanted his brother inside with him so he could talk to him out of her hearing range. There was a lot more going on than he was letting on. Tara listened intently, but all she could hear was the rumble of their voices. She couldn't ascertain what either of them was talking about. Maybe they had some news regarding Celia. She just hoped whatever it was, they reasoned it out.

* * * *

"What's going on?" Clay asked. Johnny moved further into the kitchen and kept his voice low so Tara couldn't hear them. He glanced toward the window and was glad to see it was closed.

"Celia's been spotted in this area, but the law hasn't been able to catch her. I'm worried she'll come back and attack Tara."

"Fuck it. Maybe we should hire a bodyguard for her."

"Yeah, that's what I've been thinking. I'd better go show Tara how to use this cell phone. At least we've taken one step toward protecting her from that crazy bitch," Johnny advised, walking to the door.

Johnny walked back outside with Tara's new cell phone, squatted down in front of her, and proceeded to show her that he had already programmed his and Clay's cell phone numbers into the speed dial.

He heard Clay come out on the decking and glanced toward his brother, seeing the mug of coffee his brother had brought out for Tara. Johnny stood and moved to the side as Clay pulled up a small iron table within her reach and placed the mug on it. He saw Tara smile and heard her thank his brother. Johnny sat down beside her and carefully lifted her injured leg over his lap and went back to playing with her phone so she could see how it worked. Just then he heard Clay's cell phone rang.

"Shit…All right, we'll be there as soon as we can. Thanks, Steve." Clay disconnected the call.

"Tara, we have a mare foaling out in the east paddock and she's in trouble. Johnny and I are needed to help out. I want you to go back inside so we know you're safe while we're gone," Clay stated.

"Safe from what? There's no one here to bother me, Clay. I'll be fine. Go on, go and help out. I'll go back inside soon," Tara replied.

"I'd prefer…" Clay started.

"I've made up my mind, Clay. Besides, I know how to call 9-1-1. Go and help that poor mare."

"Love you, sweetheart," Johnny said and kissed Tara, then moved back to give his brother room at Tara's side.

"Love you, too, Johnny."

"Love you, baby," Clay stated with a kiss on her lips.

"Love you, too, Clay. Now go."

* * * *

Tara watched as her men ran to the barn. Moments later they walked their horses out, mounted, and galloped off. Peace and quiet, at last. Tara sipped her coffee until the mug was empty and let her mind drift again. She didn't even feel the lethargy stealing over her before she slipped into slumber.

Tara woke up with a jolt as a loud noise penetrated her sleep. She sat up and realized she must have been asleep for quite a while because it now looked to be late in the afternoon. She looked around and saw no evidence of anyone and wondered what had woken her. Her bladder was begging to be emptied, and Tara wasn't about to ignore the call. She leaned over to grab her crutches from the decking but couldn't find them with her hand. She moved forward a little more so she could see where they were and frowned with bewilderment when she didn't see them. Tara felt a chill run up the back of her spine and settle on her nape. She looked around again and spotted movement from her peripheral vision. Celia was standing off the end of the house with her crutches in her hand.

"Looking for these, bitch?" Celia snapped out. "You think you're so high and mighty now that you're living with and fucking my men, don't you? Well, let me tell you, you won't last. None of them ever do. They will always come back to me, time and again. They've done it before, and they will again. When you're gone, they will come crawling back to my bed and will never leave it. I'll be so sad over their loss—*not*, but they won't know that. They'll come to me for comfort and won't ever want to leave. Then it will be me in this house, fucking my men. Not a little slut like you."

Tara was too shocked to reply. The woman was totally out of her mind. Tara held her cell phone down at her side and pushed the speed dial button for Clay. She just hoped he and Johnny could hear her and Celia and hauled ass to keep her safe from the psycho woman.

"What do you want, Celia? I've never done anything to you. Why did you try and run me over?"

"I was trying to kill you," Celia screamed as she walked closer to Tara. "With you out of the picture, they would be mine all over again. You ruined everything by coming back to Slick Rock. I didn't think you'd have the guts to ever show your face in this town again after what your father did."

"What did my father do?" Tara asked, dread knotting her stomach.

"He stole money from my father's business, and my daddy ended up bankrupt. My daddy couldn't take the loss of his business, so he killed himself. It's all your father's fault, and now it's your fault Clay and Johnny don't want me anymore. I'm going to make you pay, for my daddy and me," Celia screamed.

"Celia, I'm sorry about what my father did. I had no idea he had stolen money from your family. I was just a kid. I don't even know where my father is. He left my mother and me, and we ended up having to sell our home."

"Your father's dead. I killed him. He deserved to die after what he did to my family, and you're going to die, too," Celia said with a giggle as she moved closer to Tara.

Tara had nowhere to go. She was stuck with a totally insane woman bent on killing her.

Tara looked around for anything close at hand to use as a weapon. Her eyes took in her coffee mug and the small iron table it was resting on. They were better than nothing. She picked up her mug and pretended to take a sip of coffee so Celia wouldn't be suspicious of her motives. She gripped the handle so tight, it was a wonder the handle didn't break off.

"I'm so sorry for what my daddy did to your family, Celia, and I know an apology won't change anything. But do you really think killing me is going to make Clay and Johnny love you? No one can make someone love them. We can't pick and choose who we love. Sometimes I wish we could, but it doesn't work that way."

"What would you know? You've never been without love. My momma is sick in the mind from the things your father made my daddy do. Your precious daddy stole thousands and thousands of dollars from my father. My father had to take out several loans just to keep his business afloat, and when he couldn't make the payments he was so angry he beat up on my mother, and then because he couldn't live with what he'd done to the woman he loved, he took a gun, put it into his mouth, and pulled the trigger. My mother doesn't even know I exist anymore. You've still got your mom, and now you've got Clay and Johnny. I'm not letting you take them away from me," Celia yelled with mad fury as she took another step closer to Tara.

Tara drew back her arm and aimed it for Celia's head, hoping to knock the mad woman out. Celia was too quick and ducked the flying cup. Celia stepped forward and raised the crutches over her head, ready to hit Tara with them. Tara grabbed the metal table and lifted it just in time, using it as a shield in self-defense.

Tara was so involved with keeping an eye on Celia she didn't hear the pounding of horses' hooves. One minute she was staving off another blow with the metal table, the next she was being hauled away by Clay.

Tara watched as Clay wrenched the crutches from Celia, threw them to Johnny, and wrapped his arms around the mad, struggling woman. Johnny threw Tara's crutches in the house onto the floor, out of Celia's reach, then quietly took the table out of Tara's hands. The sound of a siren could be heard wailing in the distance, but it got louder as it got closer.

"Tara, are you all right? Did she hurt you, sweetheart?" Johnny asked as he squatted down in front of her.

"No, I'm fine," Tara replied then burst out sobbing.

Johnny gently lifted Tara up, being careful of her leg, and placed her down on his lap sideways. He held her as she sobbed against his chest, her body shaking in reaction to having to face a mad woman and learning her father had been murdered. Johnny cuddled her close, running a soothing hand up and down her back.

Tara's tears eventually slowed and finally stopped. She looked up to see Johnny and Clay watching her with concern. She glanced around Clay and saw the sheriff put Celia in the back of his car. Luke got in his front seat and drove away with Celia ranting in the back.

"Are you all right, baby?" asked Clay.

"Yes, thanks. Did you know my dad had been killed?"

"No one ever knew for sure what happened to your dad, baby. We all suspected foul play, but your momma didn't want you to know until it was certain. She was trying to protect you," Clay opined.

"Did you know what my dad had done? Stealing money from Celia's family?"

"Yes, we did, sweetheart. We wanted to tell you, but your mom didn't want you to know. She wanted you to keep on loving your dad, not hating him," Johnny replied.

"Well, that didn't work, because I ended up hating him for leaving me and Mom. No, that's not right. I don't hate him. I was just so angry that he could up and leave us, you know?"

"I'm sorry, baby. We wanted to tell you, but your mom made us promise not to say anything. Do you need me to take you to see Doc?" Clay asked in a gentle voice.

"No. Can you help me into the house? I think I'd like to go and rest for a while," Tara said with a hitch in her voice.

"Whatever you need, sweetheart," Johnny replied as he stood with Tara in his arms.

Tara was thankful when Clay held the door open and Johnny carried her to her room. She sighed when he helped her get comfortable and lay down on the bed beside her. She arched her head up as he soothed a hand over her head and down her back until she began to relax. She felt the mattress dip as Clay climbed on the other side of the bed, resting an arm over her waist, and cuddled her from behind. She hoped they stayed until she was in a deep sleep. She just didn't want to be alone right now and to have them hold her and make her feel safe was cathartic on her wrought nerves. Her eyelids became too heavy to keep open, and she drifted in a cocoon of warmth, surrounded by her men's hard bodies.

Chapter Thirteen

Over the next six weeks, Clay watched Tara withdraw into herself a little more each day. He and Johnny tried to talk to her to find out what was going on inside her head, but she kept changing the subject or brushing them aside. Clay knew his brother was just as anxious as he was and couldn't wait until Tara got her plaster cast off. Clay had decided enough was enough. He and Johnny planned to get Tara to open up to them and talk using any means he deemed necessary.

Clay had advised Johnny not to touch Tara intimately since she had her plaster cast on, and he knew Johnny was beginning to feel as sexually frustrated as he was. Clay knew the both of them were still going to have to take things easy with her, but looked forward to being able to move her around without the fear of her hurting her with her cast.

The day Tara was to get her cast removed dawned bright and sunny. Clay was up early, Johnny not far behind him. He knew Johnny was also anticipating a night of making love with their woman. Clay made a pot of coffee while Johnny set about cooking some breakfast. He knew Johnny was as happy as he was with the bit of weight Tara had gained since she had been a little more inactive because of her cast. He still wanted her to put on a few more pounds, though.

Clay turned to Johnny just as his brother finished cooking scrambled eggs, bacon, and toast when he heard the thumping of Tara's crutches down the hall. She was actually using her leg to walk on now, but used the crutches for stability.

"Morning, baby."

"Morning, sweetheart."

"Morning," Tara relied grumpily.

"What's the matter, Tara?" Clay asked as he brought her coffee to the table.

"This damn cast is making me so itchy it's ridiculous, and I'll bet my leg is going to be as hairy as an ape since I haven't been able to shave it. My appointment is going to come around fast enough to get the damn thing off, and the first thing I'm going to do is have a bath and shave my leg."

Clay could see Johnny was holding back a grin the same as he was. Tara was so sexy when she was grouchy. She pouted like a child, but they knew not to tell her that, it would only get her more riled up.

"Do you want some help to shave your leg, sweetheart?" asked Johnny.

"No, I don't want any help," Tara replied sullenly. "Thanks for asking, though."

"No problem. Let's have breakfast, then Clay can clean up while I help you in the shower. By the time we're done, it'll be almost time to leave for the Doc's. Is that all right, sweetheart?" Johnny asked with a gleam in his eye.

"Well, I can't very well do it by myself, can I?" Tara asked facetiously. "Sorry. I must have got out of bed on the wrong side."

"Don't worry about it, baby. We all get tetchy now and then," Clay said as he turned away to hide his smile.

Clay was surprised that their little woman was acting like a little girl. Clay could see Johnny was as happy as he was to see her displaying her feelings, even though it was a bad mood. Tara had closed herself off from them and had been hiding behind a wall of indifference. She was finally coming back to them.

Clay and Johnny drove Tara to Doc's office and sat waiting for her to come out after getting her plaster removed. They talked to each other, planning a special night for their woman. Fifteen minutes later, Tara came out leaning on her crutches with the first smile they'd seen on her face in six weeks. She had brought along a pair of sweatpants to pull over her loose shorts after she got her plaster off.

"Are you two ready to go home, because I need a bath," Tara said as she walked over to them, the crutches in her left hand.

"Should you be walking without your crutches yet, baby?" asked Clay.

"Yes. Doc said I could, as long as I use them when I need them. The more I use my leg, the stronger my muscles will become. Come on. I want to go home," Tara said with a smile and led the way to the truck.

Clay was happy to see Tara smile all the way home as she relished being able to scratch her left hairy leg through her sweatpants. He knew she couldn't wait to get into the bathtub with some scented oil thrown in to put the moisture back into her dry leg as she'd told him and Johnny umpteen times already. Maybe he would give her a helping hand.

* * * *

Tara gave a sigh of relief as she limped up the steps and into the house, heading straight for the bathroom. She plugged the tub and turned on the faucets then dribbled in some of her avocado-and-honey bath oil. She shaved her legs, sighing blissfully as the itchy growth disappeared beneath her razor, and drained the tub. She turned the faucets back on and filled the tub once more, pouring in some more bath oil.

Tara had just finished washing her body and was relaxing into the massaging bubble of the spa bath when she heard the bathroom door open.

"Do you feel better, baby?" Clay asked as he leaned against the doorjamb.

"Oh, you have no idea. I was growing an ape on my leg alone," Tara stated with a grin.

Clay chuckled with her then stepped further into the room. "Johnny and I have planned a surprise for you, Tara. How long before you'll be finished with your bath?"

"Give me ten minutes to soak, then I'll get out."

"Okay. We'll be waiting, baby," Clay said, giving her a wink over his shoulder as he left the bathroom.

Tara got out of the tub, dried off, moisturized, and got dressed. She walked into the kitchen to find Johnny and Clay waiting for her, sipping from coffee mugs.

"Hey, sweetheart. Do you feel better?" Johnny asked.

"Yes, thanks for waiting for me. What are we doing?" Tara asked.

"We're taking you for a ride, baby. You can ride with me on the way to where we're going, and you can ride with Johnny on the way back. Do you want a drink before we leave?" asked Clay.

"No. I'm good. Let's go." Tara smiled at her two men and took the lead to the barn.

"Slow down, sweetheart. You don't want to fall over and hurt yourself," Johnny warned.

"I'm just so happy that I can ride again."

"Come on, baby. Let me mount up first and Johnny will lift you up to me."

Tara waited beside Clay and then let Johnny lift her up to Clay. Clay clasped her waist while she swung her leg over the horse's neck and settled onto his lap, then urged the horse into a canter. Tara felt free again as she rode on Clay's lap. She laughed out loud with sheer exuberance.

They rode for half an hour until the creek was in their sight. Tara let her childhood memories play in her mind of her, Clay, and Johnny swimming in the summer heat in the pool of water at the end of the creek. They were such happy times. She felt her heart filling with love for her two men all over again.

Johnny dismounted first, tethered his mount, leaving plenty of room for his horse to graze, and then walked over to help Tara off of

Clay's lap. He swung her around in a circle and smiled when Tara laughed out loud again.

"I love it when you laugh, sweetheart. You haven't done much of that lately."

"I know. I've been really hard to live with, huh?"

"You? Never, sweetheart," Johnny said with a grin as he slid her down his long, hard, muscular torso.

"Come on, you two," Clay called over his shoulder as he headed for the creek.

Johnny helped Tara limp her way to the creek, and she gasped with surprise when she saw a blanket on the ground near their swimming hole and a picnic basket hanging in the branch of a tree above.

"Oh, we're having a picnic. I love picnics."

"We know, baby. Come and sit down. Let us feed you while you sit back and relax," Clay stated.

"I've done nothing but relax for the last six weeks, Clay. I need to get back to a normal routine."

"Just one more day. Please, baby?"

"Okay," Tara sighed out.

They fed Tara spit roast chicken with potato salad, tossed salad, and small bread rolls. They plied her with two glasses of wine until she lay back on the blanket, totally replete.

"Oh my. I haven't eaten so much in a long time," Tara mumbled sleepily as she put her arm over her eyes to shield them from the sunlight.

She heard Clay and Johnny moving, packing the food away, but was feeling too lazy to help. She lay back enjoying the sound of the water babbling over the rocks in the creek and the sound of birds twittering in the trees above. Life couldn't get much better.

"Tara, can you sit up for a bit, sweetheart?" Johnny asked in a voice Tara had never heard him use before. She removed her arm from her eyes and pushed herself into a sitting position.

"What's wrong?"

"Nothing, baby. We've got something we want to ask you." Clay hedged.

"Okay, shoot."

Tara looked from Clay to Johnny and back again. It looked like they were nervous to her, but she had no idea why.

"Tara, you know we love you, don't you?" Johnny asked hesitantly.

"Yes, and I love you both very much."

"Tara, would you honor us and become our wife?" Johnny asked and swallowed loudly as he drew a small jeweler's box from his pocket.

"What? What did you say?" Tara asked quietly then yelled the next minute.

"Tara, we both love you so much, baby. We would be honored if you would consent to being our wife!" Clay reiterated.

"Are you serious? Oh, sorry, of course you're serious."

Tara launched herself into Johnny's and Clay's arms as she yelled, "Oh my God. Yes. Yes, yes, yes. I would love to be your wife. But how is that possible? I can't marry the both of you, and I refuse to choose between you two."

"We've already talked about it, sweetheart. You'll marry me since I'm the youngest and closer to your age, but in our hearts, you'll be married to Clay as well," Johnny explained.

"Are you sure this is what you want, Clay?"

"Yes, baby. I'm sure. So what do you say? Is that still a yes?"

"Yes," Tara screamed at the top of her voice, joy, love, and happiness filling her heart.

The two horses in the background neighed with enthusiasm, which had all of them laughing. Tara wrapped her arms around her men and kissed them one at time. She put all the love she felt for them into her kiss, which had them growling low in their throats. Clay clasped her by her upper arms and moved her away from them slightly. She glanced to Johnny and gasped as the most beautiful eighteen-carat gold ring with a one-carat solitaire diamond was held out to her, displayed in the small box. She held her breath as Clay plucked the ring from the box and placed it on her left ring finger.

"Sweetheart, if you keep that up, we're going to strip you naked right here, right now," Johnny panted.

"So what's stopping you?" Tara replied with a saucy smile and a wink then surprised Clay and Johnny by removing her top and slowly reaching around to her back, flicking her bra open, and letting the traps fall from her shoulders. She held the cups of her bra to her chest as she removed her arms then flung it at Clay. It hit him in the face, which had Tara giggling uncontrollably with her eyes closed.

Clay and Johnny pounced. They had her stripped naked on the blanket within moments. Tara stopped laughing as the air around them thickened. Johnny moved up beside her and took her mouth with his. She answered his questing tongue and opened her mouth to let him into hers.

Tara moaned when Clay sucked and pinched her nipples, and both her men had her writhing beneath them in moments. When she arched her chest up to his mouth, Clay released her nipple with a popping sound, licking and nibbling his way down the sensitive skin of her stomach. When he was between her legs, his face level with her sex, she felt him gently spread her thighs apart and helped him gain access to her pussy by moving her thighs wider. She felt his tongue slide through her folds, and he licked her from the top of her slit to her tight, creamy hole. She couldn't prevent herself from bucking up into his mouth. The sensation of Clay stabbing his tongue into her entrance and the sound of him groaning as her cream coated his tongue made her burn even hotter.

"You taste so good, baby. I'll never get enough of this pussy," Clay said then bent his head once more.

Tara felt Clay flatten his tongue against her clit and laved it over the sensitive bundle of nerves at the top of her pussy, and he pushed a finger into her tight, wet sheath. She could feel him stroking her internal walls until she was whimpering into Johnny's mouth as Johnny plucked at her nipples with his fingers. She moaned when Clay withdrew his finger and then groaned loudly as he pushed two digits into her creamy sheath. She mewed as she felt him twist his fingers around until his palm was facing up, and he strummed the pads of his fingers over her G-spot as he kept his tongue swirling and laving over her clit, then began to thrust his fingers in and out of her cunt. He had her on the edge of an orgasm within moments. And she growled as he eased off and let her cool down, and bit Johnny's lip as Clay started tormenting her flesh all over again.

She was glad when he didn't stop this time and knew he felt her cunt ripple along his fingers when he groaned. He pumped his fingers in and out of her body faster, harder, and deeper. Tara screamed, her cunt clamping down on his fingers as she drenched his hand, mouth, and chin with her release.

She saw Clay sit up between her legs as she opened her eyes to see him grasp the base of his cock, aim for her wet pussy, and begin to work his engorged flesh into her body. When he was fully embedded in her vagina, he picked her up, lay down on his back, and held her ass cheeks to keep her still, and she knew he was giving Johnny access to her dark hole.

Tara heard Johnny quickly preparing his cock by coating it with a generous amount of lube, the slick liquid sounds reaching her ears, and then she felt him at her back as crawled up behind her. She felt him hold on to one of her hips to keep her still. She felt his cock touch her anus, and he began to push in. The sound of him growling low in his throat as her flesh enveloped him had her reaching flash point. But he held still when he popped through the tight muscles of her sphincter. It was more pleasure than she could stand. Her body was on fire, and she wanted him to fuck her hard. She knew he was waiting until her muscles relaxed and she pushed out, allowing him to push into her body until he was embedded to the hilt. She moaned once more as she tried to rock her hips back to get him to move. She felt Clay move his hips back and withdraw his cock from her tight cunt, and then as he pushed back in, Johnny pulled out and then plunged back into her ass. Her two lovers set up a slow, steady pace which had her writhing and whimpering as she begged for more.

"Oh God. You feel so good. Please, fuck me. I love you both so much," Tara cried out.

Tara saw Clay look at Johnny just before he released the tight control he had on his body, and he began to pound in and out of her body. She knew Johnny had let himself go as well, as he began to move in sync with his brother.

"Oh yes. Harder, faster," Tara yelled.

She saw Clay give Johnny a nod, and then they began to thrust their hips in a frenzy of need, a need that matched her own. She could hear Clay's breath rasping in and out of his lungs the same as his brother's as they forged their way in and out of her body. She heard Johnny groan and knew he had felt her body ripple around his cock, indicating her impending climax. She felt his fingers reach down between her and Clay's bodies and pinched her clit between his thumb and index finger. She screamed with her orgasm, her body clamping down on his, stars sparkling before her eyes. She felt Johnny remove his hand as she drenched Clay with her cum. She heard Clay roar out his release, as did his brother, and then she and Johnny slumped down on top of Clay, their bodies still spasming and pulsing as their pleasure ebbed.

She whimpered as Johnny sat up and gingerly removed his half-flaccid cock from her ass. She felt his arms around her, and he picked her up, pulling her off Clay's cock, and walked toward the creek, her head resting on his shoulder. She heard Clay following behind them. Tara was glad of the cool water since it helped reduce the heat of her body and washed away the sticky evidence of their lovemaking in the swimming hole. Johnny carried her back to the blanket, and they lay in the afternoon sunshine until they were dry. Finally, as the sun began to set, she knew they had to leave, so she got dressed, her two loves doing the same. They mounted the horses, and Tara moved over to Johnny, holding out a hand to be pulled up with him. She was riding with Johnny this time.

"I love you both so much," Tara said as she looked from Clay to Johnny and back again.

Her men smiled back at her, their love shining in their eyes.

"We love you, too, Tara," they replied together.

"Let's go home, boys. I feel the need to go to bed early," Tara stated with a smile.

Clay and Johnny laughed then kicked their mounts into a gallop. They were in a hurry to get home all of a sudden.

Chapter Fourteen

Tara slid from Johnny's lap as he brought his horse to a halt near the timber steps to the house. She ran inside and headed straight for the bedroom. She stripped off her clothes and crawled into the middle of the bed. She could feel the smile on her face and knew her men were coming to her when she heard their footsteps on the timber decking. She arranged her body artfully for her loves' pleasure. She stretched her arms up above her head until she was gripping the rails of the headboard, her chest arching up so she thrust her breasts out. She lifted her legs up, bent at the knees, her feet flat on the bed, and spread her legs wide.

She grinned when she heard two masculine groans of approval, looked toward the doorway, and gave her two men a come-hither smile. She loved the eager way they shucked their clothes and threw them to the floor. They were as eager as she was to join their bodies. It didn't matter that they only made love no more than an hour before.

Johnny reached her first and literally threw himself on top of her, and she was thankful when he bore most of his weight on his arms.

Tara stared deep into Johnny's eyes, the smile leaving her face as he lowered his head to hers. She moaned as he swept his tongue into her mouth and slid her tongue along his as they both battled for dominance. He won, of course, but only because Tara let him. She followed his lead and responded in kind as he tasted the depths of her mouth. She finally had to pull back when the need for air superseded her desire to keep kissing, his devastating flavor on her tongue.

Movement from her other side had her turning her head to gaze deeply into Clay's eyes. She felt Johnny move off to her side, giving

Clay room to get closer to her. She reached up for him as he bent toward her and met his mouth with her own. She opened up and let him in. The sensation of his tongue sliding into her mouth, past her lips and teeth, and his chest hair abrading her sensitive nipples was such a turn-on. She parried and thrust her tongue with his but still let him have control. She mewed in protest when he began to wean his mouth from hers until he was sipping at her lips. He moved back to her side, lying next to her with his head propped up on his hand, his other hand stroking against her lower stomach.

Tara felt Johnny move and turned her head toward him. She smiled as he settled himself between her thighs, lying on his stomach with his face just above her pussy. She opened her thighs wider and held her breath as he teased her by lowering his head down slowly. She growled with mock frustration, moved one of her arms, threading her fingers between the silky strands of his hair, and pushed his face into her cunt as she arched her hips up. Johnny used the strong muscles in his neck and pushed his head up, taking her hand with him, until he was looking at her.

"Oh, no you don't, Tara. We're in control in the bedroom. Clay, keep her hands away," Johnny said with a growl, his eyes never leaving hers.

Tara felt Clay clasp her wrist, pull her arm back up above her head, and gently pull both her hands into one of his, effectively manacling her. She turned toward him when she felt him sit up beside her and saw he already had the soft restraints in his hands. *How the hell did he manage that? I didn't see him move.*

Tara closed her eyes and moaned. The sensation of Johnny's tongue sliding through her slick labia had her leaking more juices from her cunt.

"I love eating your pussy, sweetheart. I could spend all day swallowing your cream," Johnny rumbled, his voice muffled against her wet flesh.

Tara wanted more. She loved the feel of Johnny fucking her with his mouth. She pushed her hips up into his face, silently begging for more. She needed his fingers thrusting into her sheath, rubbing against that special spot inside her, but knew he wouldn't give her what she wanted, needed, until he was ready. He flicked the tip of his tongue over her clit, again and again and again. She spread her legs as wide as she could and bucked. She knew if they hadn't made love earlier and he wasn't in such a good mood, that he wouldn't have let her get away with her silent demands, but she was glad they did and he was here.

She couldn't believe how much she needed him, both of them, again so soon. Just a certain look or smile was enough to have her body heating and her pussy clenching. She threw her head back and mewled as Johnny plunged two fingers into the depths of her sheath. He began to pump his fingers in and out of her body as he swirled his tongue over her elongated clit. He found her G-spot and rubbed the pads of his fingers over the spongy flesh. She could already feel the heavy warmth in her womb and her vagina walls rippling around his fingers. She growled in protest when he pulled them free of her body, her eyes snapping open to meet his.

Tara looked into Johnny's eyes as he sat up and moved his groin in closer to hers. He aimed his cock at her pussy and surged into her depths with one smooth thrust. She closed her eyes as he held still and savored the feeling of his hard flesh pulsing in her wet sex.

"Tara, look at me, sweetheart," Johnny demanded.

She opened her eyes and felt her breath hitch in her throat. All the love he felt for her was there for her to see. She felt her eyes well with tears and smiled at him tremulously.

"Keep your eyes open, sweetheart. I want to see your eyes when you come."

Tara kept her eyes on Johnny as he began to rock in and out of her body. The sensations pouring through her, the emotions welling and filling her heart as her lover fucked her, were so beautiful she could hardly breathe. He picked up the pace of his thrusting hips, gliding his cock in and out of her cunt. It didn't take long for him to have her back on the edge of orgasm. She could feel her pussy beginning to ripple around his hard flesh and he picked up the pace of his thrusts until he was pounding in and out of her body, the sound of their flesh slapping together echoing around them.

Tara struggled to keep her eyes open as her pussy clamped down around Johnny's cock, and she yelled her release. She saw Johnny's eyes glaze over, and then he was roaring right along with her. She could feel his semen spurting from his jerking cock as he pumped her full of his release. She wrapped her arms around him as he collapsed onto her, finally giving her his whole weight. She relished the feel of his body on hers as his big body pushed her into the mattress. Finally, when the need to breathe asserted itself, she pushed at his shoulder and sighed as he withdrew his now-semierect cock from her body and moved off to the side.

Tara didn't get time to even blink. She squeaked as Clay easily flipped her over and drew her up onto her hands and knees. She screamed with pleasure as he thrust into her, balls-deep, with one powerful surge. He didn't go easy on her, and she loved every minute of the feel of his cock sliding in and out of her sensitive pussy. She felt his hands grip her hips as he pounded in and out of her body. His flesh slapped against hers, and she could feel his balls connecting with her clit.

Tara moaned when she felt a warm, wet mouth suck one of her nipples and saw Johnny reach out with a hand to pinch her other nipple between his thumb and finger. She heard Clay growl as the sensations at her nipples had her cunt tightening around his hard cock. She pushed her hips back toward Clay and was rewarded when he slammed into her. He was wild and out of control. Just the way she liked him to be. She felt the warm tingles begin to gather low in her abdomen and knew she wasn't far away from her release. She used her internal muscles, clamping and releasing around Clay's flesh as she tried to milk his cum from his balls. She wanted him to reach climax before she did this time and tried her damnedest to push him over. She should have known better.

She felt Clay reach down to her slit, and he gently pinched her sensitive clit between a thumb and finger. She lost it. She yelled as her body went over the edge, clamping down hard on his hot, engorged rod as her sheath contracted with her climax. The sound of Clay's yell filled her ears as he held fast to her hips with his other hand and froze deep inside her. She felt his warm, wet release jetting up the length of his cock as he filled her with his own juices to mingle with her own. She hoped the seed from one of her men took because she would love nothing more than to have their babies. She collapsed down onto her stomach on the bed, groaning as Clay slipped out of her body. She was too tired to move, her muscles lax with satiation, but she turned her head to free her mouth from the pillow. She opened her eyes and decided to turn over so she could see both her lover's faces.

"When's the wedding, boys?" Tara asked with a smile as she looked at her two men.

Her two men burst out laughing, love and joy on their faces, and she joined in the sound of their contagious laughter.

Life couldn't get much better.

THE END

WWW.BECCAVAN-EROTICROMANCE.COM

ABOUT THE AUTHOR

My name is Becca Van. I live in Australia with my wonderful hubby of many years, as well as my children, a pigeon pair, (a girl and a boy). I have always wanted to write and last year decided to do just that.

I didn't want to stay in the mainstream of a boring nine-to-five job, so I quit, fulfilling my passion for writing. I decided to utilize my time with something I knew I would enjoy and had always wanted to do.

I submitted my first manuscript to Siren-BookStrand a couple of months ago, and much to my excited delight, I got a reply saying they would love to publish my story. I literally jump out of bed with excitement each day and can't wait for my laptop to power up so I can get to work.

Also by Becca Van

Ménage Everlasting: *Coming Home*
Ménage Everlasting: *Help Me Fly Again*
Ménage Everlasting: *Re-awaken Me*
Ménage Everlasting: *Her Norland Warriors*
Ménage Everlasting: Slick Rock 2: *Double E Ranch*
Ménage Everlasting: Slick Rock 3: *Her Ex-Marines*
Ménage Everlasting: Slick Rock 4: *Leah's Irish Heroes*
Ménage Everlasting: Terra-form 1: *Alpha Panthers*
Ménage Everlasting: Terra-form 2: *Taming Olivia*
Ménage Everlasting: Pack Law 1: *Set Me Free*
Ménage Everlasting: Pack Law 2: *Keira's Wolf Saviors*

Available at
BOOKSTRAND.COM

Siren Publishing, Inc.
www.SirenPublishing.com

Lightning Source UK Ltd.
Milton Keynes UK
UKOW041846240312

189540UK00008B/6/P